THE TALE OF HEARTS

A PARADOX OF WORDS

ANUSTHA PAL

Contents

About the Author — v

Introduction — vii

Foreword — ix

Preface — xi

1. In Nostalgia — 1

2. In The Flashbacks — 6

3. Embracing Happiness Of Smitten Hearts — 16

4. The Clumsy Winter — 31

5. Antagonist — 44

6. Everything Has Changed — 67

7. Marriage Proposal — 82

8. Division Of Life — 96

9. Begin Again — 99

10. That February — 107

11. Propose Me — 110

12. The Sweet Day — 115

13. For A Cute Bear — 119

14. Promises In Heaven — 123

15. A Love Gesture — 126

16. Cling In The Swing — 132

17. Will You Be Mine? — 137

18. First Anniversary — 144

About The Author

The author of "The Tale of hearts", Miss. Anustha Pal is a talented and empathetic storyteller who possesses a profound understanding of human emotions and the intricacies of relationships. Their writing style is characterized by its ability to draw readers deep into the hearts and minds of the characters, making them feel like they are experiencing the story firsthand.

Anustha Pal is a prolific writer and poet who has made a significant mark in the literary world over the past five years. Alongside her pursuit of a degree in Computer Science and Masters in music production, she has passionately authored numerous poetry books and anthologies that have touched the hearts of readers far and wide.

Her poetry collections, including "Scars," "Door to My Soul," "Aeipathy," "Under My Umbrella," "Flashbacks in My Cassette," "Firefly," "In the Flying Pages," "The Venue of Midnight," and "Anustha Diary," showcase her versatility and profound understanding of human emotions.

Anustha's words have the power to transport readers to a world of beauty, pain, and introspection, leaving an indelible impact on their minds. Her poems are like a beautiful symphony that resonates with the deepest corners of the soul, evoking feelings of love, loss, hope, and resilience.

"The Tale of Hearts" stands as a testament to her evolution as a writer. This debut novel promises to be a compelling exploration of love, relationships, and the human spirit. With her enchanting storytelling and lyrical prose, Anustha weaves a captivating narrative that captures the hearts of her readers.

As a poet and an emerging novelist, Anustha Pal continues to enchant literary enthusiasts with her evocative words and insightful storytelling. Her works have garnered widespread appreciation, making her a prominent voice in the literary landscape.

With her creativity and dedication, Anustha Pal is undoubtedly an inspiring figure, and her literary journey is only beginning. As readers immerse themselves in her enchanting world of words, they will undoubtedly be left longing for more of her soul-stirring creations.

Having a keen eye for observing human behavior and a passion for exploring the complexities of love, the author has crafted a captivating narrative that touches on the themes of self-discovery, acceptance, and the transformative power of genuine affection.

It is evident that the author's writing is fueled by a desire to address social issues and challenge societal norms. Through their characters' struggles with body image, social status, and the pressure to conform, the author sheds light on the importance of embracing diversity and celebrating individuality.

While their identity remains a mystery, the author's compassion and wisdom shine through their words, leaving a lasting impact on readers who resonate with the characters' emotional journeys.

"The Tale of hearts" is a testament to the author's ability to create heartfelt and relatable stories that inspire readers to reflect on their own lives and relationships. With an impressive grasp of human psychology and a gift for crafting compelling narratives, the author has proven themselves as a talented and influential voice in the world of literature. Their work serves as a reminder that love is a force that transcends appearances and societal expectations, urging us all to embrace and cherish the beauty of the human heart

Introduction

In the quaint town of Aarohan, where the seasons danced with the passage of time, a love story began to unfold. It was a tale of two souls destined to meet, entwined by the threads of fate, and shaped by the currents of life's unpredictable journey.

In this tale, we first meet Vasant, a young boy with dreams as vast as the azure sky. He was an enigma, a seeker of something beyond the ordinary. The essence of love, though unfamiliar to him at the outset, lurked in the depths of his heart, waiting to be awakened by the touch of destiny.

Across the horizon, in the same town, lived Trisha, a girl with a spirit as vibrant as the blooming spring flowers. Her laughter was a melody that echoed through the hearts of those fortunate enough to know her. Yet, beneath her radiant smile, lay the struggles of a soul yearning to be loved and accepted for who she truly was.

Their paths crossed one fateful day, like a chance encounter orchestrated by the universe itself. From that moment, something inexplicable stirred in Vasant's heart, and he found himself drawn to Trisha's infectious charm and unwavering authenticity.

As their friendship bloomed, their lives took an unexpected turn as the bond between them deepened into something more profound. But with the warmth of newfound love also came the shadows of doubt and insecurity. Vasant's mind wrestled with conflicting emotions, torn between societal norms and the purity of his affection for Trisha.

In the pages that follow, we shall witness the ebb and flow of their love, the joys of togetherness, and the heartaches of vulnerability. Through moments of tenderness and moments of turmoil, they will both learn the true essence of love—its resilience, its sacrifices, and its ability to transcend all boundaries.

Their journey will not be without obstacles. Life, in all its unpredictability, will test their resolve and force them to confront their deepest fears. Choices will be made, hearts will be broken, and the echoes of their decisions will reverberate through the tapestry of their lives.

"The tale of hearts" begins with this prologue, setting the stage for a story that delves into the intricacies of the human heart and soul. It is a tale that will explore the uncharted territories of love, guiding us through the unspoken truths and hidden desires that shape the destiny of our characters.

As we embark on this emotional odyssey, may we be reminded that love, in its purest form, is blind to societal expectations and appearances. It is a force that can heal, transform, and ignite the flame of hope within us all.

So, let us now turn the page and venture forth into the lives of Vasant and Trisha, where their love story awaits, like an enchanting melody yet to be sung, waiting to resonate with the very essence of our souls.

Foreword

In the pages that follow, you will embark on a journey of love, loss, and self-discovery—a journey that touches upon the very essence of human emotions. "The Tale of hearts" is a tale that unearths the complexities of teenage love and the struggles that come with it, written with a deft hand by an author who understands the depths of the heart.

In this world of instant connections and fleeting relationships, this story dares to explore the depths of love beyond mere physical attraction. It delves into the raw and unfiltered emotions that shape the lives of its characters, reminding us all that love is not merely a fairytale ending but a profound and evolving experience that tests our hearts and souls.

The narrative introduces us to Vasant, a young boy whose heart is restless and yearning for something he cannot yet comprehend. His journey takes a compelling turn when he falls for Trisha, a girl with a heart as vast as her spirit, and yet, insecurities begin to plague his mind. As we follow Vasant's emotional turmoil, we witness the powerful influence of society and the pressures it exerts on young minds to conform to superficial norms.

Through Vasant and Trisha's love, we are reminded of the importance of acceptance—acceptance of others as they are, and most importantly, acceptance of ourselves. We are challenged to question the judgments we make based on appearances and societal expectations, and to embrace the beauty of love in all its forms.

As the story unfolds, we witness the ebb and flow of relationships, the heartache of betrayal, and the resilience of the human spirit. We journey with Vasant through the highs and lows of his path, experiencing moments of hope and despair, all the while learning valuable lessons about the complexity of love and the choices it demands from us.

While penned by an author whose identity remains veiled, their voice resonates through the pages, reaching out to touch our souls. The characters become more than mere words on paper; they become reflections of our own struggles and desires, reminding us that the pursuit of love is a universal and timeless quest.

"The Tale of hearts" is a story that will leave an indelible mark on your heart. It will challenge your beliefs, evoke empathy, and ignite a flame of introspection within you. As you immerse yourself in the lives of these characters, may you find a deeper appreciation for the profound intricacies of love, and a renewed sense of hope in the face of life's uncertainties.

So, dear reader, I invite you to open your heart and mind as you turn the pages of this poignant tale. Allow yourself to be moved, enlightened, and inspired, for within these words lies a testament to the enduring power of love and the beauty of human connections.

Preface

In the realm of literature, stories are crafted to entertain, enlighten, and often provoke contemplation. "The Tale of hearts" is no exception. It is a narrative born from the depths of human experiences and emotions that I used to feel and I have seen around, seeking to unravel the intricacies of love and its transformative power.

As the unseen hand that guided these words, I found myself drawn to the tender complexities of the human heart. This story emerged from a desire to explore the often unspoken aspects of love, the ones concealed beneath societal facades and cultural expectations. It aims to challenge preconceived notions, to illuminate the path less taken, and to remind us of the significance of acceptance and self-discovery.

In these pages, you will meet Vasant and Trisha, two young souls who embark on a journey of love, filled with highs and lows, laughter and tears. As they navigate the path of romance, they encounter the trials of societal pressures and the insecurities that plague their hearts. It is a journey of growth, not just for the characters but also for the reader, as we are invited to reflect on our own perceptions of love and beauty.

Throughout this tale, you will find the intertwining threads of fate, choice, and consequence, weaving a tapestry of emotions that resonate with the human experience. As the characters face their dilemmas and make life-altering decisions, we are reminded that love is a force that can uplift and challenge us in equal measure.

"The tale of hearts" is an exploration of the multifaceted nature of love—the beauty, the pain, the joy, and the sacrifice. It embraces the idea that love extends beyond appearances and societal norms, encouraging us to embrace compassion and empathy for one another.

As you delve into this story, I encourage you to keep an open heart and mind, for it seeks not to preach but to spark introspection.

It hopes to foster understanding and acceptance of the diverse forms that love can take in our lives.

I am humbled to present this tale to you, dear reader. May it touch your soul, ignite your imagination, and remind you of the profound power that love holds over each and every one of us.

With heartfelt gratitude,

Anustha Pal (Author)

CHAPTER ONE

In Nostalgia

In the decade of the twenty-first century, in the big apartment of Cathedral homes in Darjeeling, Vasant was taking a sweet nap on the porch with the saddest canopy. In that villa, there are beautifully and aesthetically designed Rooms and Verandas. This is all decorated by a special person. She is the brightest side in Vasant's life, And that smitten, lovable woman is the apple of his eye, "Chitra".

She loves to attain her identity with Vasant. Their love is the symbol of Faith for their families. Some old friends of Vasant thought that she just cleverly won the heart of Vasant for his money, and Some Relatives thought that she would definitely run him on her fingers. Some just remembered them as the lovebirds, but in all, there is a beautiful relationship between both of them, where Vasant is able to feel everything that Chitra wants to express, and their understanding works just through eye contact. This is the bond that has existed between them for years.

Vasant admires all of her enchantress beauty: fair body tone, brown hair texture, the black colour of her eyes, decent height, and she is a skilled woman. When she came into his life, she became the driving force behind everything and the happy hours of Vasant.

Chitra has a sensitive personality; she gets tensed over small things. In the beginning, Vasant feels very overwhelmed by her tensed face, So he just tries to bring happiness and peace to her life. All those things start to vanish, with only the remains of angst left in her, which are very common in day-to-day life.

He takes her on long walks, and he just gives her enough time to scroll out all her issues and problems that are closely packed in the head of Chitra and then resolves them for her and clears her out. Chitra sometimes takes advantage of these culinary facts and over-cares, but that sounds like embracing a cause; she always takes decisions in favour of Vasant and what she feels is right for him. She has a highly empathetic personality. She feels everything that Vasant is actually going through and can't help but care about him.

Chitra entered the porch, woke him from his sweet nap, put the plate of fruit salad on the small wooden table, and gave him a grin gesture over his sleepy face. Vasant said, Chitra, you know this nap was so good; now I am feeling so calm, and just after that, you also bring fruits to me," and he gave her back a jolly smile. Chitra called her Maid Kusum and said "Start preparing for food, Kusum; peel off all the potatoes in the basket, then cut ginger and garlic, and then I will be there to help you". Kusum said, Okay, madam," and went back to the kitchen for further preparation. Kusum is a very talkative woman, and whenever she saw Chitra freely sitting, she started discussing with her the things that happened with her and other homely talk, and Chitra is a good listener; she hears eagerly everything Kusum tells.

So after dinner, Kusum said, Madam, what are you planning for your first anniversary? Actually, I want to go back to my village by tomorrow to meet my mother, but there is a big celebration, and Madam, I think I need to be here for your preparations. So tell me, what have you decided for me?", Chitra said, "Oh yeah, this is our first anniversary, so I want to invite all the close friends and family of Vasant and mine. I wanted to throw a big party, so I will give me a surprise party. I think we need to make a list of Vasant's close friends, Nishad and Maa. So Kusum went and asked her mother to make a list of all her close friends and relatives with their addresses. I will send them a card of this get-together; she is right upstairs", Kusum said, "Okay madam," and just ran down the stairs to reach Indra ji. Chitra started making a list of requirements and preparing a list of arrangements. Chitra made a phone call to Nishad for the list of close friends. Nishad picked up the call and said, "Hello Chitra, How are you?", Chitra replied, "Hi Nishad, actually I have called you because of our anniversary. I wanted to invite all the close friends of Vasant. So I thought you were the perfect person who could tell me about them. And it is a surprise party. Can you send me a list of all the friends with their name, address, and phone number?" So Nishad said "Oh wow, I will surely send it to you tomorrow after work; is that fine?", So Chitra said "okay," and the phone call ends.

After that, Vasant's mother, Indra ji, wrote down the names and addresses of all the friends that she knew about, called Chitra, gave her the list, and said, Chitra, I knew only a few friends of Vasant, and I didn't know the addresses of all the names that I mentioned. You make a phone call to Nishad and ask him, because he knew each and every friend of Vasant". So Chitra said Yeah, I have already called him and asked him for this list, Maa", So Indra ji started laughing and said with a jolly face "That's great", So Chitra started grinning with a jolly face, then she started making further arrangements, and then she called Vasant's brother Rishi, because he returns from his shop for lunch. So Chitra said to him, Rishi, can you help me out in making arrangements for your Big brother's and my anniversary?" So he said, "Why not Bhabhi ji, how will I help in arrangements for sure?", So Chitra replied, " I have already made arrangements for the Venue and its decorations, prepared a list of guests, and given an order for printing Cards, so you can help me by arranging Catering service as per your better idea of Catering places." So Rishi said, "Okay, I will manage it for sure, and is there anything else that I can do?", So Chitra said, "If there is any other thing that I require, I will ping you," and then Chitra arranged food on the table for Rishi, and then she went back to her Room.

The next day, Chitra goes out for all the arrangements, then goes shopping to buy new clothes for Vasant and for other family members. Rishi booked catering services, and then finally all the arrangements are complete, and Vasant does not even have any clue about it. Chitra is pretty sure that Vasant will like this surprise, and this is how all the preparation ends.

On the next day, Vasant, as a conscious and caring husband, made bed tea for Chitra and wished her "happy anniversary, my beautiful wife," then kissed her cheeks. Chitra also replied with a hug "Happy marriage anniversary, my sweet husband, and thanks for this bed tea, my love". Vasant said, "I will be back from the office early, okay, my love?" Chitra, with a jolly expression, said, "Yeah!! but please come at least before 4 p.m. because we have to go out", Vasant nodded his head and said, "Yeah!" and then he left for the office. Chitra got so many wishes from the family group that she started responding to all of them. After that, she started thanking all of them. Then Chitra asks Indra ji "Maa, what to cook for the breakfast special for today?", Indra ji replies with a smile, Chitra, make sweet porridge for this special day", Chitra replies, "Okay maa". Then Chitra went back to the kitchen to cook, where slowly the weather changed with dusk. It got a little windy, which made the weather so pleasant, and slowly time passed away. Now Chitra started getting ready for the function, where she decided to wear a black-golden elegant Silk Saree with beautiful draping style, decorate it with vintage white flower accessories, and then put on beautiful black glass bangles. Then, with light nude make-up, she puts on a small bindi, and she gets ready. Vasant came home, put his bag on the table, and reached for their bedroom. He got surprised when he saw Chitra; her beauty is melting Vasant's heart, and he said, "Touch wood, You are looking so fabulous, Chitra," and then went to see the wardrobe for good clothes, and he saw a beautiful black blazer with black pants, and Vasant really got surprised and said, "I am going to get ready," and then Vasant asked, "Chitra, where are maa, papa, and everyone?" So she said, "I have planned something for you, let's get ready to go there," and then Vasant got ready, took the car from the parking lot, and Chitra told the car driver the location. While sitting in the car, Vasant sneered because he was so happy, and they finally reached the venue, and Vasant really got surprised and happy when he saw those beautiful arrangements, and then Vasant saw all of her old friends, and that was really memorable and nostalgic for him and all of the guests there is one guest who is the nostalgia of every nostalgia, that faded all other memories and that flashback of all the memories is Trisha. At the party, waiters are serving food and drinks to all the guests, and the whole family and friends are enjoying themselves on the other corner in the lavish green and white floral prints with her hair tightly bunned. Trisha is sitting on a circular table, her beautiful smile and saree making anecdotes in the minds of people present there, a person that each eye missed. Their old friend Trisha is that beautiful lady. When Vasant saw her, she came to her place and left everyone standing there, even Chitra. It looked so unpleasant to Chitra. Then he said to a waiter, "Give Madam a chilled drink and something delicious to eat," and when he brought a cold drink and rolled so that Trisha's hands were trembling while holding the glass because of all those flashbacks in which she lived for a long time, Chitra watched that all from her suspicious eyes by standing far, and she got very anxious about this situation because she knew there was something unusual about her.

In between Trisha and Vasant, everything gets frozen, and their souls start floating in the flashbacks.

CHAPTER TWO

IN THE FLASHBACKS

There is a quaint town named Aarohan, where the seasons dance with the passage of time. It is a beautiful and developed Town, where occupations vary from Farming to Corporate, and on its outskirts is a posh colony where Vasant and his family live. In school time, when everyone loves enjoying and doing gossip, Vasant is a nerd who loves books and novels. This love for books makes him a bookworm and a topper at his school, and he also participates in olympiads, becoming a gold medalist as well. So his personality started reflecting great values. Slowly, due to adolescence, he started observing the facts of being a teenager. He was a popular guy in his class, so everyone in the class desired to be like him. Even though he is also popular in the girls' group, his notes were neat and clean. All the teachers recommend his notebooks to other students. Vasant has one loyal and crazy friend. He is the one who was The Box of Secrets of Vasant. His name is Nishad. So Vasant and Nishad do all the crazy stuff together; they know all the secrets about each other. He is the most trustworthy person in Vasant's life. Nishad is a very crazy person and just the opposite of Vasant, who keeps him in the frolic zone all the time. Because they were teenagers and because they are birds with the same feathers, Vasant started pursuing the same interest as Nishad. The serious person in him becomes a little Rebel and frolics with Nishad.

Vasant and Nishad were in the same class, So they went to school together and made fun of things at school together. So when

Nishad was going back home, Vasant asked him, "Nishad? After School hours, how do you pass your time?, cause I really got bored in the evening hours", So Nishad replied, "Vasant, I am very bad at Mathematics and English, So I take tuitions, Yashika Mam", So Vasant said "Oh, that's so great, but I don't take tuitions, cause I am already good in these subjects", So Nishad said, "Haha!! Vasant said, Do you think I take tuition only for studies? I take tuition because there are so many girls and it is so fun because we all become friends, so after tuition, we eat snacks and do fun together. That gives rise to more curiosity in the brain, and without any pause, Vasant asked Nishad " I think I have to join this tuition; we can study and do fun together", Nishad said, "Yes, brother, you are right," and then Vasant said, Okay, I will ask my mom and join by tomorrow. By the next day, Vasant also started coming to the tuitions of Yashika mam.

Now Vasant started making friends in tuition, and now all his friends are Vasant's friends. There, all his friends started admiring Vasant for his intellect; he solved all the problems of math very easily, and Yashika Mam also started admiring Vasant more than the other students. In that someone loses her worth a little bit in the eyes of Yashika-mam, that girl was Trisha, and now Trisha gets less attention from Yashika-mam. She got a little jealous about this situation. In Tuition, Mrs. Yashika usually organises small exams and quizzes. Now Trisha is performing well, but Vasant is performing better than her, and it causes tiffs between Vasant and Trisha. They always try to compete with each other.

One day, Due to some work, Vasant was absent in the tuition. So Trisha started feeling a little emptiness, but she was unable to understand why she was feeling so awkward today, so in her mind, she just recalled that everything was alright in the tuition; only Vasant was absent today, and all other things were the same. On that day, I realised something. That realisation was that she missed him and liked him. After tuition, she asked Nishad "Hi, Where is Vasant? Why is he absent today?", So Nishad replied"Trisha, I don't have any idea about that, because he is absent, also into the class",

Trisha said emotionally" So why don't you call him and ask him what kind of friend you are? You don't even ask his well-being", So Nishad said, "Why are you asking her well-being? Do you care about him? ... do you like him?" And when Nishad said those words, the shy face of Trisha turned red, and she said bye to Nishad and just ran away from there. Nishad gets her nerve, and when Trisha goes back home, she thinks a lot about that stuff, and that makes her think a lot about that. Why and how did this happen, and she just asked herself, Is whatever Nishad was saying all true? Do I like him? But I have never thought of somebody that much, may be yes or may not , oh Trisha, it is so confusing, but then why am I feeling that emptiness?" she surfs her board of thoughts on the big waves of Vasant. She just figures out that there is something undefined between them, but slowly she comes to know that she likes him.

On the next day in the tuition, when Trisha saw Vasant, With her beautiful eyes and chubby cheeks, she started making a shy face, but Vasant didn't notice because Vasant knew about his popularity among girls from the start. Trisha is obese, and she looks very Basic, simple, and kind, So he doesn't become curious about the looks that Trisha gives him. Vasant was just a little confused about why today her competitor is looking to her with that positivity and she is not making that competition and rebelling.

She is trying to focus on the Questions that Yashika Mam has assigned, but today her body language is a little clumsy. So she just can't make it. Many times she started imagining her with Vasant, but in her mind she said to herself, "Do we look perfect together? Well, I am so basic and he is okay. Okay, perfectness can't be defined by face but by love, compassion, and faith towards each other. Well, it's amazing to feel, but I don't know about him", Now the flames of love are growing in Trisha's mind. She decided to express her love to him, so the next day Trisha had planned something, so tuition had started, and Yashika Mam gave problems on trigonometry in the last five minutes of tuition. Trisha asked Vasant for his notebook, and When tuition ended, when everyone was going, she took out a flower and put that flower in the notebook of Vasant, and then she gave it back to Vasant, and he put his notebook in the bag directly. When Vasant reaches home and in the evening again opens her notebook to solve the homework assigned by Mrs. Yashika, So he found a pretty yellow dandelion, and he got surprised because he didn't have any idea who put the flower in his notebook, and in his mind he just concluded and calculated, "Who put the flower in my notebook? Question is, why the yellow danelion flower? Last time after Swati, Trisha asked for my note, Oh yeah! Maybe Trisha had put the flower in my notebook in my bag, but she is my competitor. By cleverly erranting me in discussions, Oh, may be, I suppose she likes me, but I am not sure; okay, I will clear out this confusion tomorrow, but I am feeling so rush inside me; she is so simple and fatty, although her personality is a little dumb, but she is kind, simple, and intellectual," and that is making Vasant more excited about her, then Vasant takes his phone and opens social media and tries to find her social media handle. but he was unable to find it.

so in his mind he just saying" What!!!... she is not on social media or she has a hidden acoount?, if she don't have an account, so she must be retro version woman, in this modern world, But if she has some mystrious name of her account then must be a dark horse......oh well leave it then", and Vasant put his phone down, and then he just lay down on his bed and After few seconds Mrs Indra shout out "Vasant food is ready, come down stairs and wash your hands". Vasant got up and, without washing his hands, reached downstairs and sat on the dining chair. Then he saw that delicious fish curry over the dining table, and he filled him with enthusiasm when he had a delicate smile and gaze on his face. Mrs. Indra ji observed that smile. So she started poking Vasant and said, "Oh Vasant, where are you, my boy? It feels like you are in your imaginary cloud, but thinking of whom?? ... ", and by that, Vasant felt very shy, and he suddenly changed the expression on his face and just started eating, but from inside, he was just thinking about those shy expressions that Trisha gave him in tuition, and her affection started pulling him towards her. He got the reason that,

Why Trisha trying to make the eye contact with him from previous days, and again Mrs Indra ji asked "Is there is a holiday tommorow?", Vasant said" No maa, there is just nothing but today I went to Nishad home and her monther also cooked delicious meal for me",So Mrs Indra ji said "oh you got double treat, that's why you are smiling haha!!", and then she just went back to kitchen, she know that he must be hiding something and the first thought that came to her mind is of a girl, cause she got supernatural instincts about girl and she relates it, now she conclude in her mind "I think the reason is a girl, cause Vasant never give this kind of suspicious smile before ,must be it's a God's indication for my future daughter in law, I hope so". Mrs. Indra was so fascinated by Vasant's marriage and about her daughter-in-law, so that's why she thought of her. After that, Vasant's father arrived with the green bag of groceries and some home accessories. With tired shoulders, he sat on the sofa and asked, "What's for dinner today?" Mrs. Indra should clean up the mess on the table and arrange all the things ethically. then Vasant, in his jolly mood, said, " Papa, Maa cooked fish curry for the dinner", Vasant's father also noticed that happy face, but he didn't say anything about that. Then Mrs. Indra arranged food for him, and Vasant said, " Good night, maa and papa," and they also greeted him similarly and went back to his room. His parents do some small talk, and then Mrs. Indra tells him "You know, today Vasant was blushing and smiling, and he looks so lost", So Vasant's father started laughing and said, "He is too young, Indra ji". Here now Vasant is standing on the porch and feeling the weather of the love, because love is crazy, and Vasant is not expecting much from her because this was the fourth proposal for him, but this time the girl's feelings are genuine, and the reason is that Trisha is intellectual and soft-hearted, and Vasant actually admires her truthfulness and attention that she gave to him. Vasant again goes and lies in his bed, but he can't sleep because all night he was just mesmerised by her dreams. He feels proud that a girl sent flowers to him, and with that imagination, Vasant ends his day.

The next morning he goes to school, and after school, Vasant and Nishad are walking home together, so Vasant said "Nishad, listen, I have something to tell you, but I just can't because I am feeling so shy about that", So Nishad laughs and says, Vasant, are you dumb? You are shying in front of me? tell me immediately," and then Nishad started provoking him by putting him on the pedestal of the sky, and slowly Vasant got comfortable, and then he told Nishad, Trisha, put a flower in my notebook," and Nishad got shocked, and he said, "I didn't understand, I mean really?" So Vasant said "Actually, yesterday she took my notebook in the last five minutes and she was saying that she has some questions to review, and then she put that notebook in my bag, so, of course, she put that flower in my notebook. I guess so". Nishad got excited by listening to this stuff and started teasing Vasant, and Vasant also liked the words that Nishad was saying to him for teasing, which provoked his love more and more. Now Vasant gets more fantasised by this, and after that, they both reach their homes.

Now the clocks keep moving, and it's 4 oclock, and today Vasant started getting ready so early because he is aware of the fact that Trisha likes him, and somehow he also started getting feelings for her. So in that excitement, Vasant thought to wear something more elegant and beautiful that would make a sterling impression on her. After that, he put Scent over his clothes for a better impression, and now Vasant is looking extraordinary but also wacky in terms of going to tuition; his clothes were pretending like he was going to a party. Vasant takes her mother's scooter, and he just reached the tuition, and when Trisha saw him, she got surprised, but as a matter of fact, everyone is surprised except Nishad because he knows the reason. So Nishad just teased, Vasant, is today something special?", Swati also asked "Is today your birthday?", So for cover-up, Vasant found the argument of Trisha to be very Valid or accurate, so he lied to everyone and said, "Yeah, I am going out somewhere after tuition, haha". Trisha also has a lot of excitement for this day, but she is nervous. She's very afraid that maybe Vasant will reject him, but when she saw Vasant with a jolly face and his beautiful outfit, she just guessed that he was in her favour. Now tuition has started, and Mrs. Yashika gives the Question to solve. Trisha intentionally dropped her pen, pretending to be insane, and tried to see Vasant by stealth, then tried to make eye contact with him. But Vasant is dedicated to Solving his Questions by intentionally ignoring her because he wants to make her feel confused. Trisha started becoming anxious about this situation, and now she is trying again and again. Suddenly their eyes meet for once, and Vasant just wants to stop for her eyes, but he sees Nishad is looking at him and just giving a funny smile. Vasant shys away and starts looking into his notebook again. Nishad watches all that scenario keenly, turns towards Vasant, whispers into his ear, and says, "I am watching all those hints that you both give to each other from your eyes". After some time, tuition ends. Vasant, without looking at Trisha, just go away with Nishad. So Trisha started walking with Swati, and while they were both walking together, Swati asked Trisha "Are you in an affair, Trisha?", Trisha said, "Well, I have something to say. Actually, I like Vasant. I have put a flower in his notebook, but he didn't reply to me", Swati said, "Oh my god! Something like this has happened in front of my eyes, and I don't even have any clue about this. Well, Vasant is a nice guy for you, Trisha. I just pray to God that they will make the decision in favour of my Trisha", Trisha also started praying to her god. On the other hand, Nishad asks Vasant, Why don't you say anything to her in reply? She was looking at you and you are just ignoring her; that's not a good thing to do with a girl. What's in your mind? Just tell me. So Vasant replied, "Actually, I am just confusing her, because I want to see that love in her eyes, and I am just noticing all the things that she is doing for me. That small thing and all those things show her faith for me. Nishad burst out into laughter and said "You are so Stupidly amazing, Vasant. I just like the way you guys talk indirectly", Vasant passed a shy smile to Nishad. Now both lovers are on the pedestal of realisation, and what other people are saying is that they are making bridges of their closeness and just realising more and more.

-->Next day

Now with the glory of a new day, they went out for the tuition again, and the road is full of thoughts, and thoughts are occupied by love. Everyone just reached the tuition, and all students just settled down. Then Mrs. Yashika ran upstairs in a hurry and came into the tuition hall and said, "Sorry students, I am a little bit busy today because tomorrow will be my Son's birthday, and for the celebration, I have to make arrangements, but you all already arrived here. So Vasant, can you please handle all these students and explain to them the Pythas theorem on my behalf, and then Trisha, you will teach them trigonometry formulas. Is that Okay?", Vasant and Trisha replied "Okay mam" and now they both felt Frisson, but this was destiny; for him, she also gave the task to Trisha, and Vasant also asked himself "Is she my destiny?". On the other hand "Trisha feels very shy, that she got the possibility to work with Vasant", they both are making jolly faces and explaining. Now they started feeling some kind of attraction towards each other, and even now the obstacle in front of Vasant was her feelings of little conflict regarding her physique. He messed up in calculating her beauty factors and overall personality, and he faced a lot of issues on this, but somewhere he is under the umbrella of love, and this is something that he just can't disagree with. Finally, he ignored all of them and decided that tomorrow he would confess his feelings in front of her. With those three magical words, he just walked over that conflict and made plans accordingly. He said to himself "Cause I love her a lot, I am accepting all those drawbacks of her, and I will make changes in her that are required to make her look perfect". He spent the whole night making this decision. But now there is a big yes on his tongue, a sign that shows that he agrees. The next day after Tuition, when In the dusky evening, roads get covered by dry autumn leaves and there is some kind of aroma of Nature sitting over the wind, Vasant, holding shyness over his cheeks, said to Nishad, "Hey brother! Today you have to go alone, because today I am going for Trisha", so Nishad said with a small grin, "Best of luck, my brother," and he just Vanished like an evaporated water droplet.

After that, Vasant started following Trisha, and she was walking home with Swati. Vasant was waiting for the disappearance of Swati so that he could flow her beautiful River feelings to her. Trisha has no idea that Vasant is following her because he's not clever enough, but Swati has noticed all that, so after some time she becomes aware of it. So a conversation gets started between Trisha and Swati. Swati said "oh my god, Trisha there is someone who is following us ?", Trisha get scared and said "Really, okay reach home fast", So Swati said"Oh my dear, at least turn a little and have a look", and When she saw the person who is following them is Vasant, her face blush and her jolly face tells everything to Swati, so Swati said "I think he wants private talk with you, so okay now I have to go", Trisha with hiding her excitement said "okay Swati", and Swati change her route and leave her. from there Trisha started walking alone and now she has strong feelings that, he is coming for her to confess something, but suddenly a thought make home in her mind that "Is he coming to insult me for that flower or may be whatever she is thinking is just a myth and he just coming to reject me, or he have problem that I try to make eye with him and that make him feel embarrased", so she get afraid with her negative thoughts and just started making big steps, Vasant have noticed that she fasten her speed and she's just dissappearing from his sight, so Vasant also started making big steps, cause now Trisha is alone so Vasant shouts "Trishaaaaa...", and Trisha stops on her place and look back and then Vasant walk towards her . Trisha said "hello Vasant" and just started looking down, and they started walking together. Then Vasant said, Hi, Trisha, how are you?", Trisha said "I am not fine", So Vasant asked, Why?", So Trisha said "I love someone but I didn't have courage to tell him", So Vasant saidTrisha said "hello Vasant" and just started looking down, and they started walking together. Then Vasant said, "Hi, Trisha, how are you?" Trisha said, "I am not fine." So Vasant asked, "Why?" So Trisha said, "I love someone but I didn't have courage to tell him." So Vasant said, "Don't be afraid, Trisha, be brave. Now that you have said this much, then say this also. Now obliquely, they both understand each other's feelings, and now Trisha is sure that he must not be rejected here. So Trisha said "There is a beautiful park near this place, just walking distance; I guess it just takes five minutes", So Vasant said, "Yeah sure! why not". They both went to the park, and when they reached there, Trisha showed him the beautiful tulip garden, where all the space was covered by tulips, and the place was fully covered by the beautiful aroma of tulips. Near the flowers, there was a park bench. So Vasant asked, Trisha, can we sit there?", Trisha said, "Of course, Vasant, I really love to sit there with you!" and they both sit on the park bench. When they sit there, suddenly a mysterious silence enters their talk, and then Trisha looks into his eyes. She puts her fringed hair behind her ear and, with a keen smile, says, Vasant, I really like you", In between them, there is mysterious silence again, and Vasant is just looking into her eyes. Trisha was full of chaos because Vasant was not saying anything, and then Trisha said, Why are you not responding, Vasant?", With a shy smile, Vasant then held all his complex aside, making emotional jolly gestures. Vasant took her hand and said "I just want to say that I love you", and a wind of love started running in between Them, and then in response, Trisha gave a faithful emotional smile that made the moment very special for them. This is a love story that has started in a beautiful dusky evening that is leading to the beautiful moonlight and a starry heaven. This is how the love story between Trisha and Vasant started.

CHAPTER THREE

EMBRACING HAPPINESS OF SMITTEN HEARTS

The day comes with this strange love that Vasant and Trisha start to experience, and every moment has wings, and they just fly in this sky of love. These strong and huge feelings are like a galaxy into themselves. Vasant's horoscope is in his favour. He finally possesses a beautiful heart. For them, classes became a love triangle. When Vasant sees her again today in tutoring, he feels that he has known her for years and that love and affection are looking into her eyes. In the tutoring session, Vasant and Trisha were sitting next to each other, and on the other side of Vasant sat another girl. All the students were solving the questions. This girl was having difficulty solving a particular question because the language of the question was so typical that it could not be understood. So she asked Vasant, "Can you help me to solve this problem? I am not able to understand these problems". So Vasant said, "Yes, let me see!" and he started to analyse the problem. In the end, Vasant started to tell her how to simplify the problem, and they started to talk in a low voice. When Trisha hears this whisper, she becomes jealous and pinches his arm. Vasant cried "ouch" but could not say anything more. Because he liked the feeling of jealousy in Trisha's action, it is reflective. This created an emotional bond between the two. After class, Vasant sits near the huge peepal tree and waits for Trisha to come outside. When she comes outside, he asks, "Trisha, are you still jealous?" She started giggling, and when Vasant saw her doing that, he also started smiling, seeing her so happy.

They met every day, and their trust in each other grew day by day. They got to know each other better and started caring for each other. Late-night calls, dates, the same cup of tea, long walks—there are many things they enjoyed in their relationship. On this list, one particular thing that everyone wants to know is the first kiss. Nishad, Swati, and all the other people want to know. Did it happen or not? The curiosity to know is fascinating for everyone because curiosity is part of growing up. The key factor in any adolescent story is the curiosity to know and to experience. Throughout the circle of friends and at school, everyone knows that Vasant is having an affair with a girl named Trisha, so everyone is curious about it, but Vasant has not gone that far yet because he wants her to feel comfortable first. But all the classmates asked Nishad if Vasant got his first kiss, and Nishad told everyone he did not know, but Nishad thought to ask him. Nishad's curiosity got even bigger. After class, when he was walking with him, he asked Vasant, "Brother, can I ask you something?", Vasant said, "Yes, why not", Then Nishad asked, "Did you get your first kiss?", Vasant felt so shy and said, "Brother, I am in a relationship with her; what do you expect from me?"", Nishad again asked, "What should I guess from this relationship? You did it or not?", So Vasant replied with a giggle and said, "You can think what you want", So Nishad said, "Oh, it means you are not to say smart boy; well, it's okay; tell me whenever you want".

One day, after class, they were walking together, and clumsy Vasant said, "Today I am very tired, Trisha, because I have been working on a project for a week". Trisha did not like his tired face and said, "Vasant, can I ask you a favour?", Vasant said, "Why not, my dear? I am your companion". Trisha suddenly said, "I want a kiss", This woke up the tired eyes of Vasant, and then Vasant, with a jolly smile, said, "Why not, Trisha, but we have to find a good place for it. Which one do you prefer?", Trisha became shy and said, "I just do not know", so Vasant said, "Okay, let me decide", and he started thinking about the best place for it. Vasant remembered the idea of "The sweet-hearted restaurant" because that is very remote and rarely do people go to that restaurant. So Vasant said "Okay, let us go". Vasant takes Trisha to this restaurant and reserves a table for her. They sat down there, and then Trisha noticed something strange, and she asked Vasant, Why are there no other guests except us? Is this place really very remote?" to which Vasant replied, "Well, I did not assume so, but this open green courtyard and beautiful decoration of this restaurant look amazing, and the great and most important thing is that we also have privacy. Just a chef and a waiter who are in the kitchen right now, so Trisha, are you comfortable with that?", Trisha came forward and kissed Vasant spontaneously because she was a little shy at that time, and then they both kissed. Trisha became very nervous, and Vasant made a face as if he had committed a crime.

This was so different from what was supposed to happen. After some time, the waiter came and served the ordered dishes. Trisha and Vasant grab all the food without paying any attention to morals, and after they finish eating, Vasant pays the bill. Then they go back, and by chance Nishad meets them, who sees that Trisha and Vasant are out together. Nishad asks" Vasant and Trisha, what's up?", Trisha, with a thief's heart, says, Actually, we just want to eat something", and Nishad feels they are hiding something, but he doesn't interfere with their privacy and says, "Okay, I'll accompany you till home".

Nishad and Vasant left Trisha near her house. After that, Nishad and Vasant walked home together. Vasant put his hand on Nishad's shoulder and said, "I want to eat something spicy; let's go to the market." With a jolly face, Nishad too put his hands on his shoulder and went to eat at their favourite snack bar, where they like to eat kabab, but it was so crowded and the place was closed today. So When they reached home, Mrs. Indra greeted Vasant and Nishad and asked, "How are you, Nishad?". Nishad replied, "I'm fine, aunty",

In between, Vasant said to Mrs. Indra, "Maa, we want to eat something", to which Mrs. Indra said, "I haven't cooked anything yet, but I'm preparing the ingredients for Pav Bhaji. I love to cook for both of you. Don't worry, I'll cook in a few minutes; Bhaji is already prepared", Nishad and Vasant felt happy inside, and Vasant said, "Sit here and make yourselves comfortable". After a few minutes, the bhaji was ready, and she served it to Nishad and Vasant, who were both hungry and reached for each other's plates. Mrs. Indra served them the sweet ras malai that her husband had brought for the family in the morning, and they enjoyed it. Suddenly, Vasant remembered the project proposal that had to be submitted by the day after tomorrow. For their project, they needed someone who was very intelligent and had great knowledge and practical skills, so Nishad and Vasant thought Trisha would be the perfect partner for this project. The next day in class, Vasant asked Trisha, "Hey Trisha, can you help me? I've got to give a presentation; Nishad is my presentation partner, and I need someone else who knows about these important topics," to which Vasant showed her the topics. After looking at the topics, Trisha said, "Yes, I can". Vasant replies, "I knew you were better at this subject", to which the innocent Trisha hides her smile and says, "Yes, of course". Trisha has been trapped by love, and Vasant has been trapped by her innocence, and they make a promise to each other. After the project, they go for ice cream. Afterwards, Trisha goes to a cyber café with Vasant and Nishad, where they collect all the data for the presentation. After completion, they all go to the school library and start the presentation together. The work is divided into two parts, with Vasant working on the first part and Trisha helping Nishad with the second part. Slowly, but with consistency, their presentation gets ready. The next day, they have to give the presentation in the form of a speech in front of the class. So they both start practising in front of Trisha, but they're both not fluent enough. They spend the whole day preparing, and the next day they give the presentation, but Trisha is worried about Vasant, but somewhere she is confident in Vasant but not in Nishad. In the evening, Nishad and Vasant met Trisha, so they thanked her for her efforts on them.

The next day was stormy, the cold wind blowing with the sweet aroma of the earth. Vasant was thinking about how we'd go to class today to meet Trisha and Nishad, but suddenly it started raining and it also became windy. It was such pleasant weather, and Vasant was eager to meet Trisha. So Vasant texted Trisha that she must come for coaching. Mrs. Indra asked, "Vasant, why are you going outside in this crazy weather?" He replied, I've got to go, Maa; today's tuition is very important for me". Vasant went out wearing a raincoat and reached tuition, and then Trisha also reached Tuition with her yellow umbrella at the same time. When Trisha saw Vasant in his Macintosh, she started giggling with her small teeth. Vasant asked, "Why are you laughing, Trisha?" Whereupon Trisha said in a funny accent, "You look so funny in that green Macintosh, like a turtle, haha!" Then Vasant got shy; he took off his Macintosh and sat down next to Trisha. Mrs. Yashika came up and saw that there were only three students today. She said, "I don't know why students skip class for petty things; they all have excuses, but the students who are here are really very hardworking. You all came here despite the rainy weather, so we have to start now, because the gift of life is only there if you keep your eyes open", she began to teach, sharing her experiences and her story.

After class, Vasant and Trisha walk together, the rain stops, and the weather becomes calmer. The pleasant weather after the rain gives the two a feeling of allure; they look lovingly at each other and can feel the love in the air, and the background noise just disappears for Vasant and Trisha, with love songs playing in the background in their headspaces. It's so strange how love comes from the universe, reaches your soul, and you find someone. After that, they just make small talk with shy smiles. Trisha suddenly stops and says to Vasant, "Look over there, on that cardboard box." Vasant looks around and says, "What's so special about that black cardboard box?" "Nothing about the box, but see, there is a beautiful green leaf lying there. But there is no tree nearby. How can this leaf travel such a long distance? Can you imagine that a leaf can travel a long distance even without legs?" said Vasant. "Why do girls notice everything?" and then both of them started laughing, and Vasant just stopped to find the logic behind the leaf, and he said, "According to my concept, before it rains, there is a windy storm. Maybe that's why this poor leaf travels a long distance; it gets from one place to another with the wind, and then suddenly it starts raining, and this poor leaf falls on this black box and stays there because of the water, and then, as you can see now, the weather is alright, so it stops here, and that is how, without having any trees, this leaf sits over on this black box. Maybe that's the story of that scenario," Trisha said, giggling. "Great discovery!" In response to this sarcastic acknowledgement, Vasant said, "Great philosophy, Trisha!" With this conversation, they became more comfortable expressing the unique things and ideas that were floating around in their minds. From behind, Nishad spoke, "What a love story! The boy is an explorer and the girl is a philosopher. What a fitting god!" Vasant said, Don't tease her; she is my lady. Okay, brother", Nishad laughed and said, Okay, brother," and just joined them.

Nishad always interferes in his love story as a friend, but the feminine soul in Trisha sees him as a villain or troublemaker, and he always jokes on her. In her mind, she thought Nishad, why don't you mind your own business and just interrupt us". Vasant realises everything by the angles of her face. Vasant always felt so embarrassed for his friend Nishad. He said to Trisha, "He is our best friend; don't make such an unhappy face; he is just joking." Nishad realised and started going back, so Vasant stopped him and said, Nishad, come back; you're my best friend, and she was just thinking of something else." He turned around with a childish face and said, "Vasant, you know we're best friends," and hugged Vasant. On the other side, Trisha felt really jealous about this. Vasant felt very bad and said to Trisha, "Never treat him like that because he's like my brother, okay Trisha," and with a selfish expression she said, "Okay, sorry Nishad," and they ended the topic, but somewhere Trisha has stored this point in her memory of the headspace. and she'll remember it for a long time. That point can affect her in the future. Trisha didn't like the fact that Vasant gave Nishad priority over her. Vasant found this fact a little bad because he thought it affected her brotherhood, but on the other hand, the kind of love she feels for him is unconditional, and Vasant realised that he's treating her wrongly. He thinks about it a lot and gets his mobile phone and texts her, "Sorry for the rude behaviour, Trisha", and when Trisha reads this message, she gets full of happiness. And this is how this beautiful day ends.

The next day, Mrs. Indra made delicious "Aloo Parathas" in the afternoon, and when Vasant saw this, he thought he'd bring this for Trisha, and she was impressed. So Vasant packed some parathas for her in his tiffin and put them in his bag after class, with a sticker that said, "This is for my beloved Trisha", and when Trisha saw this in her bag after class, she was surprised and said, "Thanks, Vasant, for bringing me this delicious food", and gave him a big smile. She was so happy about it that she said, "Vasant, I love eating these parathas with tea", whereupon Vasant took her to a tea stall, and they started eating these parathas and enjoying the whole meal. Then Trisha asked, "Vasant, which one do you prefer, tea or coffee?" Vasant said, "Although I like coffee more, but I also like tea, and what about you?", Trisha said with a strange smile, "I love tea because I feel the native thing, in the tea only ", and Vasant agreed with her and said, "You're right, but I still like coffee more," and after finishing the whole meal, From the side, some tuition-mate friends of Trisha saw them eating food together, they came towards Trisha and started humiliating her, and a girl said, "What are you eating, Miss Fatty?" Trisha felt very bad but said nothing, and then another girl came forward and said, "You both look so unbecoming together", Vasant, to teach them all a lesson, said, "Trisha, you are beautiful, everyone present here is just okay, and listen ladies, she will be a slim and fit woman in a few days", and hearing this, they all went back with angry faces and felt so jealous that Trisha has a supporting partner. After that, they left the shop, and as they were leaving, Vasant asked, "Are you okay, Trisha?", Trisha said, "I am very happy; you know, when you were standing there for me, I felt it", Then he asked, "What about training?"" Trisha said, "I will try", to which Vasant said, "If it is difficult for you, you can also go to the gym", to which she got annoyed by listening to that and said, Well, I will think about it", to which she said, "Oh, Vasant, it is getting too late now, go quickly", to which they came home with long strides, and then by making big steps, they reached home, and this is how the sweet day ends.

The next day, when they return from tuition, Vasant says to Trisha, "Trisha, you know that I love everything about you, and if you maintain yourself and work on yourself, then I will be proud of you." Trisha asks, Vasant, do you think you really love me?" Vasant said, Of course, Trisha", to which Trisha says, "If you love me, then you must also love me physically, mentally, and emotionally, and accept me as it is; don't change me". Vasant said "I love you unintentionally for your everything; you are worthy to me in any physical state; your physicality doesn't change the way I approach you; but it is my responsibility, Trisha, to draw out the best from you; and if you can look slim, why do we have to accept this one?", and both disagree with each other. Trisha said, "Everyone has their own point of view, but at this point we can't, Vasant, try to understand," to which Vasant said, "Okay, drop it, Trisha, I feel so restless," to which a cold war started between the two of them.

but they both behave casually, and slowly it turns into a knot in the thread of their relationship. In Trisha's mind, it just gets fixed that she is not perfect for him, and she starts facing all those insecurities, and from there, she is fighting for a long time. In Vasant's mind, it's fixed that she's not going to change her for him. But Vasant is so stubborn that he will change her with time, but first he wants her to have all faith, and then he will ask him again. and he assures her that he will give her the best version that she can become, and this only happens when she realises the importance of health and fitness. but it is something that comes to you on your own. Now their thread of relationships has a few knots that they just can't ignore. Slowly their friends come to know about the gap between both of them, so some girls try to make a home in the heart of Vasant, but they just can't, because he just doesn't want that, and Trisha is already in safe hands. Even though they have an argument, he still takes care of her, and she is in safe hands. After some time, they both get over this and just move on from this argument.

So one day Trisha said "Vasant from a long time since we didn't go on dates, can we go out this weekend, so Vasant said " I have some plans to execute but still I will make time for you", Now Vasant ask, so Trisha what you are wearing for the date, So Trisha asks "do I have to wear Traditional or western ?", So Vasant said, " I haven't seen you in the pure Traditional clothes, why don't you wear something ethnic?", Trisha said" okay Vasant", then she went home and Mother of Trisha was has gone to the market so, Trisha find it as an opportunity to dress well, cause know her mother is not here to ask anything like where you are going, so Trisha go into her room, open her wardrobe and start looking over all the ethnic clothes, she really get confused, with the chaos she said " ahh there is nothing good to wear", then her eyes fall over her yellow embroidery kurti, she wears that kurti with her jhumkis and with a touch of black small bindi, she gets ready.

Now near home, at some distance Vasant is waiting for her, and she makes a phone call to him and asks him, "Where are you, Vasant?" Vasant, tells Trisha, "Trisha, I am standing at some distance near a stitching shop near your home, that Moti Tailors". She replies, Vasant, please go away and stand in that previous market location; I will catch you from there. Because that Tailor knows me and my mother very well, it will create a problem for me. So with a non-impulsive, dull, sad smile, Vasant said "It's okay, Trisha, and cut the call without listening to a second word", and Trisha feels that he gets offended by her statement. So she went out and closed the door, and she started running to reach him. Vasant, when he saw Trisha in yellow Kurti, in a big step and in fast speed coming towards him, his heart became jolly again, and he lost all despair. When she reached him, Vasant asked, Trisha, you are looking beautiful, my love, but why are you coming so fast",

So Trisha said, "Actually, I thought you were waiting for me from a long time, so I just ran away from home at speed. But I also want to say, sorry Vasant, I didn't mean that, I just said that because if he saw us together, maybe he can create a problem for us and our parents aren't aware of the fact that we are dating, so it will create problems for our future and I love you Vasanth but it is truly hard actually cause I want to marry you," so Vasant said "don't worry Trisha, I am understanding it all but seriously you looking pretty today", then suddenly Trisha get frozen and she make a scared face. Vasant felt there is something happen so he asked, "What had happened?" , "Vasant said Actually, I saw a lady going in the opposite direction; she really looked similar to my mother, so subconciously, it will happen" said Trisha. Vasant by making a laughing face said, "you know if I get scared, haha! ". Trisha said "Okay, okay, let's change the topic; I am fine ; now it's alright?", Vasant said "Yeah". Vasant stops at a medical store and buys some tablets. So Trisha asked Vasant, Vasant, what happened? Why did you buy those tablets at this time", Vasant said "Oh, actually, Trisha, these medicines are for my father; I know when he comes after work he forgets to buy them and then he skips today's medicine, so I have been searching for hours and now I have finally found it.", Trisha said "Oh, you are a caring person, although", Vasant said, "Thank you, Trisha, for understanding me. I love my family and you, and I am doing everything to make you all happy", Trisha said "I appreciate your efforts for your family". he then keep driving .

Now they Reach a beautiful Cafe that Nishad has recommended to him. All the cafes are decorated with beautiful, colourful lights, giving them a glamorous look. Vasant and Trisha really liked the cafe outside there. After walking a few steps, Trisha saw an ice cream parlour. Trisha asked Vasant, "Do you like to have ice cream?", Vasant replied, "Why not? You know I am an ice cream lover", So Vasant asked Trisha "Which one do you prefer, because I am buying a chocolate and vanilla cone" Trisha said "I love mango-bite", so they bought and started eating ice cream. Trisha said "Oh, I guess I am having sensitivity in my teeth", Vasant laughed and said "Trisha, you don't use good toothpaste, I guess, haha", Trisha, making an innocent face, said "Vasant, don't laugh at me. It's embarrassing", Vasant said, "Okay, my love". Then Vasant said, "Trisha, you know why I love this cone? Because it has yummy chocolate in the bottom of the cone. This is why I buy this cone". Trisha nodded his head and said "Oh, Is that so?", In reply, Vasant also nodded his head. After that They enter the cafe and everyone is just looking at Trisha, cause she's looking gorgeous in yellow Kurti, but Vasant doesn't like that everyone is looking at her, he just makes faces like a protective guy and take her there in the porch of that beautiful cafe, and asked Trisha " So what would you like to have dear?", Trisha said " well order something of your own choice otherwise you will argue with me and then order something of your own choice", Vasant felt alot but infront of the waiter he didn't want to say anything so he said "Trisha order something of your own choice, my love", Trisha said "okay, well then can we order pasta?", Vasant said "okay", So the waiter asked, "Pesto or alfredo ?", Trisha said "Pesto", then Vasant said "No, Trisha Alfredo is better", By listening to different opinions Waiter ask again then Vasant said to Trisha "We Order Alfredo", the waiter said "okay sir", Trisha said to Vasant" now you can see that you have to order of your own choice of food, then why you take my opinion", Vasant replied with a suprised face "Trisha I have ordered from your choice, I just choose category of own choice but the dish is of your choice", Trisha said with giggle "yeah you are right, Vasant", and Trisha said "What do you think about life that you going to spent with me?", Vasant said "I know life is unpredictable but still I want to make you mine", Trisha said "yeah , I also try my best to make you mine, I make every effort that is in my hand", Vasant see her dedication for him and it's impressive for him, these arugument and small talks are taking them close to eachother. So they finish their food, enjoy it, and it starts getting late, so Vasant drops Trisha at home, and he also goes back to his home. Trisha, when reaching home,her mother, Mrs. Sen, said "Oh, my daughter, you are looking beautiful, but from where are you coming?", Trisha said "I go to a friend's birthday party", Now Mrs. Sen has started noticing changes in her daughter; she notices she is happier nowadays, uses more beauty products, and a lot of her things have changed now. She is pretty sure that something is going on, but she is too busy with her household duties, so she won't have time for this. She has one daughter and one son, which means Trisha has one brother who is older than Trisha. So one idea made a plot in Mrs. Sen's mind: she said to Son, Take care of your younger sister Anubhav", He said Maa, actually, I was so busy nowadays", She said to Anubhav "I know you are so busy in your job, but still you can take care of her, Anubhav", So he said "Okay, Maa, I will take care of that; you just don't worry for her". As per Mrs. Sen, who is the mother of Trisha, she knows that Trisha is an innocent girl, soft and sweet by heart, so Mrs. Sen is always protective towards her because she knows even small things can break her. For that sake, Mrs. Sen has taken every decision of her life since childhood, and she has never fought against any one of them because she is so obedient towards her mother. So Mrs. Sen said to Anubhav, "I am noticing some changes in her behaviour, and I don't want her to fall on the wrong paths, so Anubhav, you have to be Attentive towards her", Anubhav said Mom, don't worry. She is my sister, and because my father is not home, I am the man of this house, and I will take care of her". Mrs. Sen got relaxed when Anubhav said that, and she said "Thank you, my son!".

Now Trisha reached home late ,and she saw Mrs. Sen cooking food in the kitchen. Suddenly a heavy, loud sound came into the ear of Trisha. That sound is the voice of Anubhav. He said Trisha, why are you so late today?", Trisha replied, "Sorry brother, actually I just went out with Swati for a friend's birthday party. That is why I came late, but I will take care of it. Then Mrs. Sen didn't say, Trisha, come here and help me in the kitchen" but Trisha said, Maa, I am coming within Fifteen minutes just by washing my face and changing my clothes. Trisha went upstairs into his room, changed her clothes, washed her face, and just laid on her for a few minutes to give rest to her body. She started thinking about today's date, which was so special for her. She's getting a very amazing feeling about today. Then she went downstairs to help her mother. Mrs.Sen is cooking biriyani rice and gravy, So when Trisha came, she said to her, Trisha, help me in the preparation of food", Trisha started washing vegetables and helping her. After that, Mrs. Sen, Trisha, and Anubhav were having lunch together, and Mrs.Sen said, Trisha, you are looking so beautiful today; you have grown up, my little daughter". Anubhav also said "Yeah, Trisha, when I saw you in the kurti, I also felt so", So Mrs. Sen said "I think we have to start searching for your groom", At that moment, Trisha thought of Vasant, gave a shy smile, said Maa," and just went away from there with a shy face, and Mrs. Sen and Anubhav also started smiling. Trisha went back into the room and started looking in the mirror, and she found everything great, and then she said to herself Yeah, I was looking pretty, but I think I need a makeover for Vasant; oh yeah, Nisha has a great knowledge of beauty products and how to use them; I think I have to ask her about this". She made a phone call to Nisha, and Nisha picked up the phone call and said "Hi Trisha, no call from a long time, now how do you remember me after these days", Trisha said, Hey it's not like that Nisha,and how are you?", Nisha said "I am good and what about you?", Trisha said " I am also great, butI have seen your photos from Swati, where you have done very light and beautiful makeup Will you help me out and let me know about your products and brands that I can recommend, and even how you use all those things. I have an idea of using everything but I didn't haveny idea that what I just know is the perfect one", Nisha said "Why not, Trisha? It's great that you think about that, because, you know, every woman needs to know at least how to make up and cook ", Trisha said, "Well, there are other things also, but yeah, somehow you are right. So Tell me, Nisha", Nisha first recommended the brands and then started telling her, "You know, Trisha, I love makeup and I want to become a makeup artist, but my parents don't allow me, so I just keep it as a hobby for now, but if you have asked me, I am feeling so happy in telling you. Because you are a beginner So let me introduce you to the products that you can use. First, choose the foundation that suits your skin tone; don't use any other foundation that doesn't suit your skin. Other times, it will whiten your face and make you look ugly even if everything else is good enough. Before applying foundation, apply primer to your face; it will give a long-lasting finish to your makeup. Then, apply foundation over it. You will need brushes and a sponge to spread it evenly on your face. then apply concealer below your eyes and spread it then apply concealer below your eyes and spread it evenly. "Trisha, are you getting me?", Trisha said Well, it is so confusing, but yeah, Slowly I am understanding it all. Can you teach a little slow?", Nisha replied "Okay, well, I can try", So you will get that primer, foundation, and concealer?", Trisha said, "Yeah, you can move forward. Nisha started telling again. "Now you need contour to define facial features; apply it carefully, okay? Then you have to work on your eyes; now for decorating them, you need eyeliner, mascara, and eye shadow, so first stick tape at the end of your eye at an angle. Oh, but it is hard to explain; are you getting Trisha?" , Trisha said "Yes, I am getting you, because I already have a little idea about that", Nisha continued, "Then apply eye liner carefully; it takes time, but slowly you become perfect. then Apply mascara to your eyelashes, then slowly start learning how to apply eye shadow and search for the colour that makes your eyes look beautiful. That depends on you, so this is the most basic procedure. I know you don't get it all at once, but start trying these all; you definitely understand", Trisha said "Yeah, thank you so much, Nisha, for telling everything in this depth; I really get a better idea now how to do that", Nisha replied, "Welcome, dear. I also feel really glad while I am telling you all that, Trisha. If you really want to learn that, so begin on your own and also learn from others, and over the internet also", Trisha said "Okay, Nisha, I will try, and I will also come to you to learn better" and Nisha said "Yeah, sure, okay Bye!!" After the talk, Trisha and Vasant started texting, and after the long talks, they said, "Good night," and they both went to sleep. The next day after her work, Trisha started learning new skills, and she is very happy that she is learning something new in her life and that she is also thinking about the things that are present in her life.

CHAPTER FOUR

THE CLUMSY WINTER

After a few days, autumn has just fallen all the leaves from trees, and slowly, cold winds started flowing into all the places. This is the arrival of winter when all the farms are covered with collards and rabi crops are already harvested, and now in every home, slender onions with green tops, pods, and mustard greens have become common, and now consumption of tea is increasing at every house—one cup of tea that makes all the difference. People started pruning trees for the wood because, slowly, mist was covering the area. and cold winds are blowing in every place except the tropical and coastal regions. There is a difference in the temperature, but everyone is feeling cold.

At the home of Trisha, all the family is sitting around the fire, and the whole family is enjoying it because Trisha's father, Mr. Sen, has returned from his job on holiday. so all family is sitting togther and discussing the events that happened with them everyone telling their anecdotes, where Mr Sen started telling "You all know, we all officers in freezing temprature, sometimes get duty in forest areas, so there we do campfire and cook something there and get heat from that and it is rough but a amazing feeling to a person like me", Trisha said "Oh wow papa, that is so intresting", so on otherside Mrs Sen started giggling and said "there are so many amazing things in which your dad is brave, but still your father is afraid of lizards", and everybody started laughing and then Mrs Sen said "Trisha bring sweet potato from the kitchen and put it in the ash of this fire", Trisha said "Okay mother", and go inside, in that time Mr Sen tells to Mrs Sen "How Mature has our Trisha become now", Mrs Sen said "yeah, she is so mature now, I am thinking about her marriage,even I am noticing all the changes in her, I don't want she take any wrong step in her life", Mr Sen said "Yeah I am also concerned about her marriage, and I have already selected a guy for our Trisha",Mrs Sen get surpurised and said "Whom and you haven't tell me about him yet?", So Mr Sen replied with a jolly face "Do you remember my friend Lieutenant Raghuveer ?",Mrs Sen said "Yeah", so Mr Sen said " his Son also joined the army, one day Raghuveer just mentioned that his son is going to join the army then I will tell him about our Trisha. About her simplicity and affection, after graduation within two three years, when it will end so he will fixed there engagement, but rightnow we don't disturb her. Cause I don't want that she loose her focus". Mrs Sen get full of jolly and said "oh now I am tension free, you know I am so tense for Trisha from few days and I was thinking our daughter is very innocent in respect to this society, how she will going to manage all of the things, even I asked Anubhav to take care of her Sister, but this make me feel so light, and I am very happy" and then Trisha comeup with sweet potato, Mrs Sen put it the fire that now turns into an angithi and after roasting them, all family eat sweet potato and enjoyed the day with delight.

The next day when Trisha came home after tuition, she goes sit inside her blanket, Mrs. Sen called Trisha, and Trisha shouted from her Room, "Maa I am sitting inside the blanket and I am not going to go outside", Mrs. Sen said "Trisha come out dear I am having something for you", so Trisha come out from her blanket and go towards Mrs. Sen, she put their hands back and said "I have something in my hand for you, any guess", Trisha become very curious and she doesn't want to guess, so she said "Maa please tell me fast, it's so cold if there is something good so I will stay otherwise I have to go back into the blanket", Mother opens her hands and show her wool and Mrs. Sen said "let me teach you how to knit a sweater or cardigan" and started telling about the knitting. Trisha started learning something new, so she is very happy about this. Mrs. Sen started teaching now, and she said, Knitting a sweater is very unnerving because you are just beginning, but in actuality it is very easy if you follow the process correctly by following a pattern, and when Trisha has learned these basics, I will show you some different patterns, okay?". she said "okay".

Mrs. Sen said: "When I a learning kniting for the first time so my mother tells me "That one day laado you grow up into a women, so you have to learn kniting to impress your mother in law and at that time I was thirteen, in my mind I feel that may be maa is saying. so I was just imagining but it didn't actually know how it feels, even at that time I really don't know anything about womenhood, but see today i have a daughter of age eighteen and Similar to my mother, see I am also teaching her the same things " and she suddenly go deep down into her thoughts and started reminding and telling me about her experiences with her mother. She started telling Trisha, "We used to live in a small village, where we have a small house; we don't have the facilities that you are adoring. In my village, winter comes with fatty cotton quilts, but we really enjoy them. I have a friend, Rajeshwari, who is always there to play with me. We go out and collect the soft pebbles, then over the soil, I draw blocks, and we play Hopscotch, where, just like a ladder, we have to move forward and complete that ladder of blocks. It's so fun to play those games with her. It was really something beautiful that I hate because it is disappearing now; now I don't see girls playing that. Like us, with my parents, we also sit around the fire to enjoy ourselves, and you know, in between that, we do all the work by sitting there only; we usually skip all other things just like your father", Trisha made jolly faces, and that gave a hint to Mrs. Sen that she was interested in her talk. Then Trisha asked, "And what about school, maa? Maa, what do you do in your winter breaks? Do you also not go to school when you feel cosy inside the blankets?" , So Mrs. Sen said "Actually in that era Education don't get this much importance and for women, it is not even evaluated worthy" and with a giggling face she said "my friend Rajeshwari comes at our home and ask for me and then she comes to me and started shouting that do fast, otherwise we become late, so Then I just get activated and started running for school and when I refused for going to school, my mother said to her that Rajeshwari leave, you also don't go to school today and she goes back to her home cause I am not going, So innocent of her" and when Trisha hear that, she started giggling and asked her mother "Mom if don't go to school daily why you sent me on academics daily?", she said "ahh well, listen, young lady, you know era keep changing but the thing that never going to change is cruelity towards women and you know my daughter an illetrate women are treated wrost by everyone in this society. Somewhere, as per my observation, Our education system is not perfect, but the key to your empowerment goes through this path. You have made yourself find the correct path. Trisha, you know your father and family, including me too. We are all waiting for your marriage somewhere. It is the right thing to do, but on the other hand, I want to see my daughter as independent and someone who is not just someone's wife and daughter, but somewhere she is something so that she will get the respect from society that she deserves, and she has to be prepared for all the ups and downs and to make the right decisions on her own. I also want to see my daughter living in a beautiful house and having a family, but on the other hand, I also want that you have some identity in this big world, so now I used to think that the doors of exposure are only reached on the basis of your education, so try hard, my daughter, do you get it, Trisha?" Trisha replied "Of course, mother", but from inside, Trisha felt it so difficult when she heard her mother's words.Cause they are sounding very contradictory. These words were sounding like a bitter truth to her, and she was realising that in the dreamy world that she had imagined with Vasant, She just ignored these things and kept forgetting all of herself for him, and at that moment she decided that she must change a little by little so that she can focus on him and studies, both equally and also for better time management, but somewhere she just fluttering in the dreams of marrying Vasant and started thinking about that life that she was going to spend with Vasant. Her Maturity ends over her love, and now she is trying somewhere, but she is under his love; somewhere she is facing the bitter but true words of her mother and her adolescence, making her fall into dreams again; for her love, she becomes blind; for her faith, she sometimes just becomes an autumn leaf and falls down, but just like spring again, it just revives. With Increasing love, her patience is decreasing, but she is still coping with her hormones. She said to herself, "I am trying to unlock the doors to success, but still, there is something that is not working." Now she just realised that she is leaning more towards her love and Vasant and less towards her goals, but she didn't want to make the changes because she felt happy in that. and she just knows what is right for her, but she is still unable to make up her mind about that path, so she decided to keep things as they are and let things happen to her with the flow of life. and in sorting out all that stuff, the day passed by. After a few days, the date sheet for exams appeared, and Trisha got worried about that and started taking feeling anxiety. Vasant noticed her anxious face, so he said to Trisha, "Hey, don't worry about that; I am with you, Trisha.

On the next day, as they are both getting closer in the days that are passing by, their parents are able to feel the changes that are happening in their behaviour and workflows. Most of the decisions Trisha makes concern her mother, but nowadays she asks her fewer things. Her mother feels that she is so busy on her own, but she has no clear idea about that, so she just ignores all those facts. Now life was taking turns and attracting Vasant because, after the exam results, Vasant was at the top of the leading board. This makes Trisha happier than Vasant, and her belief in his goodwill is also increasing, but this is something more proud for Mrs. Indra Ji. When she came to know that Vasant had topped the all over the state, she felt proud and decided to reward his kid. She ran towards the temple and prayed to her god. She started thanking her god and made a beautiful confession in front of him. After that, she called his father and told him about that, and on that day, Mr. Raghav became so proud of his Son. On the other hand, so many girls get obsessed with this fact that they want to approach him. Vasant still doesn't have any ego for this victory because he is just searching for something else, but somewhere he is also feeling proud. Trisha passed in the first division, and that is also an achievement. Mrs. Sen is also very happy with the result of her daughter, and she forgets everything in this happiness and says to Trisha, "I was thinking that you were not good in academics, but you proved me wrong. She says, "Yeah, mother, but my friend Vasant has really helped me throughout all the exams, and you know, ma'am, he topped at State level", So Mrs. Sen said, "Oh, that's really great, my daughter," and Trisha went back to her room. And that day became the fortune of Vasant.

So Vasant goes out with a few of his friends, in celebration, where everyone is happy for passing the highschool, but cause Vasant is now the topper of his school, all of his friends started pulling his legs of Vasant by poking and teasing him the nerdy boy, intelligence freak and smart, by representing him as a smart personality, and in between that one of his fellow said " you are a topper, so you are smart, but I don't think you are smart enough to take the shot of this whisky", where Vasant know that he is somehow triggering him but his adolescence feel so insulted about this fact and then everyone started laughing at him and that hurt him, and he said "I can easily drink that, it is not something tough but I just don't want", he said to Vasant "oh really, oh you are a good boy I can understand", then in this adolescence pressure he just started looking over the glass of wine, and suddenly at that moment Trisha called him suddenly, so he came into the corner to talk, Trisha ask "hey Vasant, how are you?",Vasant get little nervous cause he is about to drink whisky, cause he knew Trisha get angry over this fact and this is not the right what he is actually doing, he just want to confess it now on this phone-call, but then he just freak-out by the thoughts that he is imagining and he lose the courage of saying that and he changed his words and he tell Trisha " hey Actually I am out with friends for a party, I will be late", Trisha said "Vasant and what about my party?", Vasant replied " we shall go out tommorow somewhere , okay my love?", Trisha replied "yeah okay, I am so happy, and take care !!", and now Trisha cuts the phone-call, now he have that whisky in one hand about which he is regreting, cause he felt that he have responsibilty of Trisha, and in that crucial time if he become an alcoholic, so who will take care of Trisha. So he went back and refused to drink and sat aside and started thinking about her mother's words to do that; she hated his alcoholic aunt, and it also hurt her, so keeping that thing in his mind, he was just overwhelmed. This time, when all his friends provoked him, he just smiled and refused; now the love of Trisha is dominating over other things. So Vasant said "Okay, now I am ordering food; everyone, please tell me your choice of food", Then they ordered one kadhai paneer, chapati, hot tea, a small bowl of noodles, and Muradabadi Biriyani. Everyone eats a lot and finishes all their meals. When Vasant went out to pay the bill, everyone else started discussing Vasant and the effect of that phone call. One friend said, I think he got the call from his mom, and that is why he refused to drink. Then one guy spoke out: These were the effects of Trisha's love on him; I think that phone call was done by Trisha. Then everyone started discussing rumours about them. This is the hot topic there. now that everyone knows that he is a topper and that his personality and intellectual status attract everyone. This love story fascinates everyone. Vasant came back after paying the bill, and everyone just stopped talking and went back.

After coming home, Vasant sat near the window of his room, and he was feeling special that he took that step for Trisha, so he made a phone call to Trisha and started with a simple hi, but told her everything about the party in detail and about that incident, and then he said, I just don't know about the European countries and how they manage to be non-alcoholic, but also because there is extremely cold weather, it gives them a reason to drink. But here, most people started drinking and slowly made it their habit, and they ended up in a bad situation, and I don't want that. So I have decided not to even touch it; my ethics are not allowing me, and this moment makes me feel special about you. Trisha said with a smile, "I am so happy with your decision, and It's really an honour for me", and after some small talks, they cut the call.

After that, Vasant started thinking about plans for tomorrow and employment because he is so dedicated to his work. his optimism towards his dreams and the things he wants to achieve in the future. He has a grey-out diary with a shiny golden flower design for the border, where he usually writes about his journal, goals, and personal life. He tried a lot of things, but he just has failure on his hands. He is too stubborn for his goals, and he never lets himself stop because of problems. A kind of person who is inclined towards a solution This time he just planned everything very well and also focused on academics because, for a better college and place, he started preparing for good scores. On the other hand, Trisha, who is in blind love with Vasant, was too focused on things related to him to shine in his eyes. She was learning new things, with acedemics.like looking for enhancing beauty-related products and learning how to use them so that she can look better to him. She also normally studies her academic stuff. Mrs. Sen, when she entered Trisha's room for cleaning, noticed that on her dressing table were some beauty products. These things first stung her eyes, but then she thought that she was in her adolescence, so maybe she got influenced by someone, so she just said nothing to her, and her mother said to Trisha, Trisha, after doing your work, come into the kitchen to help me." Okay, Trisha agreed with a nod of her head. Then, after some time, Trisha goes into the kitchen and starts helping, but she is looking a little distracted by something else. Mother put her dialogue into a giggle. "Trisha I think you not cooking food ", Trisha surprised and said " Maa then what I am cooking with the help of a spatula?", Mrs. Sen replied "thoughts" and started laughing and Trisha also started laughing and said "you are saying anything randomly maa", then after completion Trisha said "Maa this okay dish is ready, I have put the remaining grocery in the refrigerator, okay, now I am going to watch that drama", she goes into the veranda and open the TV and start watching a drama where Mrs. Sen also loves to watch that drama and her curiosity awoken again and she joined Trisha and started watching drama together, in the drama the situation comes when main characters are lovers and they are separating somehow, due to the current scenario. The soft heart of Trisha has started sobbing, and she just cried, "Oh maa, why does that happen?" in a very sad and disappointed voice.

Mrs. Sen replied, "Because love is not fair enough to do with a random person, this was her wrong decision. I know that guy is great, but still, it is wrong in the eyes of society", Trisha said Mom, do you really think that, mother? But you know in actuality how good he was", Mrs. Sen said "My daughter, but I know how things reflect in society and how to think.", She then tried to explain to Trisha the reality of love that she had figured out from her own experiences. Mrs. Sen said, "Love does exist in this society, but this world will not run only through love; it needs resources, money, and hard work. and the people who spend a lot of time in love are not able to maintain that, so how can they give a good future to their children? So in real life, these things usually don't work out." Trisha found herself in the wrong situation and with the wrong character, and everything started questioning whether whatever she was doing was right or not. So Trisha asked, Maa, what about you and papa", So Trisha said "Because you know that your father and me, we both aren't able to experience a lot of time together, but still, after our parents chose us for each other, and till now, we feel the same for each other, and we are raising you and your big brother proudly", Trisha again asked, Mother, I have a question for you; will you answer it for me? Mother said, Yeah, sure, why not? Trisha asked, Are you sure that the way that you love Papa, she also loves you the same? Mrs. Sen found this question very critical to ask, but she answered, Of course, my soul knows that your father still loves me the same, but because we have a lot of responsibility, we are so busy and unable to express that love to each other, but after your marriage, I just feel free. Trisha said in fun, What about a brother? Mrs. Sen replied cheerfully, Including him also. Trisha felt excited when she heard about her brother's marriage. Mrs. Sen said with confidence, "I am going to find the most beautiful and cultured girl, because you know your brother's aura; I also deserve a cultured daughter in law," and she laughed. Somewhere, Trisha understood that there was something that her mother wouldn't tell her, but she just ignored everything because she had now started a discussion about her brother's marriage. Then Trisha asks her mother "What should we wear for Anubhav's marriage", Mother replies, Because you are the groom's sister, you have to look special. Would you like to wear a beautiful lehenga?" Trisha says, Maa, I want to wear a heavily crafted lehenga of any elegant colour.", Mrs. Sen says, Yeah, you look so elegant and beautiful in lehenga, but Trisha, why don't you reduce some weight so that you just look perfect? Trisha, you have to start by today to look your best". Trisha agrees with the comment of her mother, and somewhere she is also feeling insecure at the same time, but putting her fragile heart aside, she said, Maa, do I have to join the gym?", Mrs. Sen replied, "It will depend on you; if that is what you actually want, you can also start daily exercise at home". Trisha said, Yeah, I think about it; I will surely try my best". Mrs. Sen sneered and asked Trisha, Why do you ask such questions to me?", Trisha cleverly replied, "I just asked casually, mother, and also because we are watching that drama, our thoughts are just conflicting".

After that, suddenly someone knocks at the door of Trisha's home, and when Trisha opens the door, she finds her father standing with bags and says, "I am home, Trisha." Trisha got very excited about this surprise visit from his father; he sat down on the couch, and then Mrs. Sen saw Mr. Sen sitting over the couch. She was full of happiness at that moment and also surprised because she didn't have any idea about that. They hugged each other, and Mrs. Sen and Trisha also sat on the sofa. Mr. Sen asked "How are you, my daughter?", Trisha replied, "I am a good father, and what about you? Father replied, "Yeah, I am good and also happy because I have seen you for months; where is Anubhav?", Trisha replied

He has been to the office; maybe he returns near seven", Father said, "Okay, this is also good, that he is doing his job with hardship; well, I am going to change my clothes". He goes upstairs. In all that, Trisha reminded to call Vasant because now she is free to do so. and she was sitting up on the roof and talking with him. Anubhav went back home, and he went upstairs to take a breath. When he saw Trisha talking to Vasant, he shouted in a low voice, Trisha, what's going on? Do you have any explanation for the person to whom you are talking? Trisha got shocked and panicked because that happened suddenly. She felt a frisson in her heart because somewhere her brother was going to know about him, and on the other hand, he may not like this and tell her mother. She just becomes speechless, and then again Anubhav asks "Trisha Maa and Papa are not here, so will you tell me about what's going on?", Trisha held some courage in her heart and said "I like a guy named Vasant; he also likes me back", By breaking her words, suddenly Anubhav burst out in anger and shouted at Trisha, "Are you mad? You even have any idea who that guy is? What is his caste and background?", Trisha felt numb and scared by his words, so she said "He is from an upper caste like us, I guess", Anubhav, in anger, said, "What does your guess mean? Are you thinking your life is a joke, loving a guy about whom you don't have an idea, you are so childish, he said that he loves you, and you believed, don't you think about your parents' concern, at least take concern from me, don't you think about your family and their respect, while taking such a big decision", Trisha's eyes are down, and she is standing in embarrassment, and with watery eyes, she said, "I am really sorry, brother. I am sorry for doing all of that secretly, without your concern, but believe me, he is the most loving and trust-worthy person I have ever met, and I know he doesn't let me down". Anubhav said "Give me his phone number, and I am going to see him tomorrow and drive him up by a wall", Trisha really gets scared by the words of his brother. She was getting nervous, so she called Vasant and told him everything that happened. Vasant said, "You don't need to worry, Trisha; I will handle this situation and your brother. I will try my best to convince him. and slowly the day passed by. The next day in the evening, Anubhav reaches them after tuition, and when Vasant saw her brother, he got a little scared, but he controlled his fear and started giving himself confidence. Anubhav said to Trisha, Let's go" and then he takes both of them to the nearby restaurant to have some talk, and then he takes them to a separate place where no other person is sitting nearby, and then he starts asking Vasant, What about your profession, Vasant, where do you live, what your parents do, and how much time you spend with my sister?", So Vasant started telling him, "Sir, I knew Trisha from last year, and I really love her. Professionally, rightnow I don't have any occupation, I am studying yet, and I am pursuing further education. Besides that, I am working in workshops, and I have different plans and approaches for the future that are not yet complete, but I am trying. My Father is a businessman; he has many shops, and my mother is a housewife. I also have one sister who is in third grade. Anubhav said "Are your parents aware of her?", Vasant said "Not yet, but I will let them know about her soon", Anubhav said "First thing, a loser like you doesn't deserve my sister, and your parents don't even know about her if they refuse, so who will take her responsibility?", Vasant said, "I am taking her responsibility, and within a few years I get employed, and then I will tell him. If they refuse, then also I am not going to leave her". Anubhav said to Trisha, "you need to think about him again; it is your decision, but I don't think Maa and Papa get to agree on this; now it's your choice to stay with him." This talk will hurt the ego of Vasant, and somewhere inside he feels frowned, but he controls all of that because he is Trisha's brother, so Vasant knew if he said anything wrong, he has power and authority to take Trisha away, so he sat with his scar, but somewhere he started hating him as a character in his life. All the respect for Anubhav has disappeared with his words. Anubhav said "Okay, so when are you going to tell your mother about him?", Trisha replied "I need time, brother", so Anubhav said, "Okay, take your time". and he leaves Vasant and Trisha, pays the bill, and leaves from there. Trisha, although she doesn't like the words that he says, likes that Anubhav doesn't separate her from Vasant, doesn't even tell anything to her mother, and leaves all the situation on her, and Trisha thought somewhere God was helping her. and she smiled and saw Vasant and held him, and by seeing her happy, Vasant also became happy, but in actuality he was not. he go back to home by holding some tension in the lines of his head and the moment he entered into the home, Mrs Indra got to know that something went wrong, cause he don't showing any happy expression and he is little bit silent, and she thought there is something unusual with his son so she decided to serve him food first and said " Vasant you back my son have your meal", so Vasant by putting a fake smile said "okay mother", cause he knew if he refuse to eat the food , so mother will ask so many question regearding to not eating the food, so he sat on the dinning chair and mother arrange food for him, he eat all the food and put the plate in the sink and said " mother I am little tired today, I am going to my room", Mrs Indra nod her head and said "okay my son, yeah the lines over your head are telling that you are tired", he nod his head to agree and go back to his room but there he is unable to feel that peace, so he go to the rooftop terrace to take some fresh air and cool down and there he sat and started realising everthing and started accepting everything. Some ego is still left in some corners of his heart, but now that he is feeling better, he has decided that he will not recall the bad incidents and just ignore them. and he said to himself "Don't tense Vasant; one day I will talk to Maa and convince her, and then I will marry her someday", Then he made a phone call and talked with her about her happiness and small talk again, full of enthusiasm, and got all his courage back. Then they discuss everything regarding the day, and that sad day ends with some positivity from Trisha and some great hopes. and that's how the rough day ends.

CHAPTER FIVE

ANTAGONIST

Now the clock was changing its time. They are together, but slowly time is changing everything at its own pace, and it seems that the thread of love has started to unravel. Their strengths started becoming their weaknesses, and time changed their way of thinking and their personalities as a whole. Vasant's world started changing a lot, and Trisha doesn't like the changes. So slowly, that started becoming poison in between them. In this stage of life, from teenager to adult, they are becoming adults, and adulthood doesn't work great for them. There are several realisations that are felt now. Friends of Vasant started teasing him by fat-shaming his girlfriend, Trisha. Vasant always takes a stand for Trisha, but somewhere from inside he is feeling hurted and incompatible. Their incompatibility becomes the reason that everyone only stalks them. Vasant felt the need for the training that Trisha required. Slowly, by small pinching, he tries to convince Trisha to reduce her weight to become fit. But Trisha started taking that point so personally. She doesn't want to change herself. For her, the definition of love is to get acceptance at any condition or at any time. That is what she wants from Vasant. So because of their different thought processes, there was frequent conflict between them. In that phase, everything in between them is running so fast. This time they are looking at each other, but not in the same way or with the same love. It feels like for Vasant, the foreverness in their relationship is not working out. He felt like a donkey, pulling the carriage with the weight of

Trisha.

This time when things are unstable, suddenly a wall grows between them, a wall that is made up of factors like incompatibility between each other, because now Vasant has started watching compatibility in someone else, and this happens when a heavenly beautiful girl, who holds modernization in her comes; thoughts starts growing in between them as a wall, because when a third person comes between the two loving halves, distance automatically increases between them. She joined the same tuition classes. Her name is Shefali. Similar to her name, she just looks like a beautiful flower, So everyone is fascinated by her. Her morden views stuck in every head, and that makes her different from others. Her status and lifestyle are very attractive to every teenager's eyes. She has a socially active personality, which is why she has accounts on many different social media profiles. She named her social profile as "Social Butterfly,", where she is too popular for her feminine beauty. She has everything that a teenager is fascinated by, but in acedemics she has an issue with mathematics, and that's why she has joined the tuition classes. There are so many facts about her that make her amazing, but the most important factor is her beauty and clothes. So when tuition started, she came to Mrs. Yashika. In the first class, she came in a simple, serene top and pants that made her look so different and classy. Every day she wears something beautiful, and Vasant is also impressed by her personality. Vasant felt that attraction, but he didn't see her like that because he was already committed. Slowly, the void parts of Vasant are getting covered by thoughts of Shefali because she only talks to Vasant. The reason for her talks is that Vasant is an intelligent and smart guy, so she likes him in a way, and she also interacts only with him. where next sitting Trisha saw that closeness between Vasant and Shefali. So Trisha started hating Shefali.

After class, Trisha started taunting him, and she said "Oh, somebody's eyes are rolling today in the class". Vasant replied "There is nothing like that; whatever you are thinking, you are talking just rubbish, and your imagination is going in the wrong direction". Trisha started pinching him again and again. Vasant is now feeling so irritated, and he yelled at Trisha and said "Silent, stop creating drama". Trisha's fragile heart started crying, and she became sobber, and in a sober voice, she said "Oh, so now my things look like a drama to you", So Vasant explained, "Trisha, listen, I am not saying you to stop talking; I am saying you to stop blaming me and creating false connections". Trisha replied "I have seen how close you both are sitting, and the way I have seen, it must be that you are interested in her; all your desperate feelings are catching your face, and I can see it". It decreased the patience level of Vasant, and now things started getting serious little by little. Then they both started arguing with each other, and their arguments increased the negativity that they were both unable to control. So as usual, Vasant said "If I have eyes on anyone else, why am I investing everything in you". Trisha replied, "Oh, now you come to the investment and the money. You want to show me now how much money you have spent on me. Do you think I am a gold digger, living on your money?". Vasant again shouted and said, "Today, why are you taking all the thoughts in the wrong direction? You are behaving like a maniac woman?", Trisha said. "Oh, now I am a maniac; how can you be so rude? You keep yourself busy; I always wait for you. Sometimes I have doubts that maybe you talk to other girls, but then I think maybe you are busy. But today, when I see you talking to that girl, I no longer want to rely on you. Why does she always talk to you? There are so many students, but she talks only to you. Even though I am absorbing the day she joined the class, you talk to her, and it makes me feel left out." Vasant stopped his panicked mind, tried to calm down, and said, "Okay, It is my fault, and by tomorrow I will not go to talk to her, and I don't have any idea that you are feeling left out, but now I will take care." Trisha, with cruelness, replied "You must not talk to her". Vasant maintains his calmness after that fight, but there is still a cold war going between both of them. where Trisha is overly possessive and skeptical and Vasant is too open and has a lot of female friends, so that's why they both get conflicted.

whenever Slowly daily recognising Vasant, Shefali also feels attracted towards him, so now she tries to find excuses to talk to him, and Vasant tries to ignore her, but her attractive way of talking, her body language, and her overall personality don't allow Vasant to just ignore her; he explains and tells her whatever she asks him.

One day Trisha didn't came to the tuition, and on that day, Shefali saw that her clingy girlfriend was not present, so Shefali thought that now she had a chance to tell him that she liked him. slowly she started discussing about tuition, so Vasant said "you feel comfortable in tuition", so Shefali replied "although everyone stalk me, still it's okay", so Shefali said "by the way are you on social media?", where Vasant said "yeah I am everysite of social media, I don't like to post but it is good for creating contacts", so Shefali ask "okay then give me your ID name and handle of facebook and talkingbees", Vasant feeling so excited and said "ah, I am least active on facebook, but I am usually active on talkingbees", shefali said "me too, but cause I run a page of fashion and dance over facebook, so I have to post alot, so I am active on both". Then Shefali sent a request to both of his accounts. Vasant gets the notification, but Vasant doesn't give any reaction. Shefali liked this quality of not being so clingy and said Yeah, I sent you the request; accept that later", Vasant nodded his head and said "Yeah, I will", and then Shefali asked, "How is Trisha? Why is she absent today?". Vasant said "Well, I don't know, because today I haven't talked to her". Shefali looked at her with sceptical eyes and said, "Why?, Is everything alright?", Where Vasant said Actually, she was having heavy arguments with me, and then that argument converted into a fight, and now in that case, I am not talking to her". Shefali, showing sympathy, said, Vasant, well, I am a stranger still, but I want to know what is going on between you both; maybe I can help you out", When Shefali said those words, Vasant found her an understanding person, and then he told her about her relationship. Shefali saw a chance that sparkled in her eyes, and she sat with Vasant and listened to everything. Over social media, Vasant saw her modelling art pictorial videos, where she was looking glamorous.

From small talks to conversations, Vasant and Shefali became best friends, and slowly, Trisha started feeling jealous of her. Because as a friend, she loves her more than Trisha, and he talks less to her. Trisha is the better half of Vasant, but the remaining half is Shefali. With the passing of time, Shefali becomes a better place for Vasant. She understands her, and whenever Vasant has a fight with Trisha, he goes to her place. Trisha always gets hurt by their closeness. So from day to day, the arguments and fights have increased between Vasant and Trisha. Somewhere now, they are together because of promises. Vasant is a thought-oriented person. He was stubborn and so sure about his words. So the words that he gave to Trisha say that he wanted to fulfil his promises, so he doesn't leave her. Like that, slowly things keep moving, and fights and arguments happen too, but still, after a few days, they came back to each other.

Now slowly, with the pace of time, Vasant reached the twelfth grade with good marks, and that is why Vasant's father got very impressed with his marks and decided to send him to a Big and reputed school. Now he fills out the form for a reputed school that is in the city area, out of their district. Because his home was so far from his School, he convinced his father to rent a room near his school. Vasant came to the new school, So Nishad felt so left out because they were best friends. So Vasant said to Nishad that he also gave the entrance exam, where Nishad also got selected with the least number of marks. but still, they were so happy because Nishad was selected. Now they have started living together, and Vasant cames to tuition only two days a week when he goes back home, so Trisha and Vasant now have very little time to spend together. Shefali's house is near the outskirts of that city. So whenever she finds a chance to meet him, she takes all of them as an opportunity. She sometimes even went to his room. With the changing atmosphere, Vasant started exploring different things. His adolescent feelings started triggering him more and more. Now changing their friend circle exposes them to all the things that are restricted, whereas illicit videos are more convincing for them. Now the desire to make

Trisha an idol woman has captivated Vasant's mind. Because he knew otherwise, he started looking for things in another women. Trisha, when exposed to the meaning of beauty in depth and her desire and surety for Vasant's existence, is a great lover of inner beauty. With her grooming and knowledge, she tends to get stubborn in her thoughts, but Trisha changed her approach and started daily exercise at home. She really wanted to do it for Vasant. After tuition in the evening, she called Vasant to tell him about her plans, and Trisha made a phone call to Vasant. when Vasant picked up the call and said "Hello". Trisha said, Vasant, I have changed my mind, and I am starting to exercise from now on." Vasant said, Wow, today my love has impressed me". and with small talk, their call ends. Shefali's call is on hold, and now Vasant picks up the call of Shefali and Nishad in the backend, noticing all the things. He starts teasing him and says, "Oh my god, two girlfriends, Vasant; have you won both of them in a lottery?". where Vasant said "Hey, she is my female bestfriend , okay!!, your jealousy have caught words". So Nishad said, "So why are you blushing more on Shefali's call? You don't blush on Trisha's call". Vasant was surprised because Nishad had noticed a face expression that he wasn't even aware of, so he said "Really?". Nishad replied "Yes, my friend, even her eyes also shine when she looks at you; even I have noticed she is finding ways to talk to you; don't you think she is giving a variation of excuses that are weird?". Vasant said "Well, yeah, somewhere you are right, but I never noticed, but...as a friend she can, it's her previledge". Nishad said, "Oh, now you are also on her side; there is something." Vasant said, "There is nothing," and this is how Vasant realises that for him, she is more than a friend now. Then he thought about Trisha, and started thinking and talking to himself, and said, "Do I really like Shefali? But My love is Trisha. Do I really want to make changes for her? Or, now that she is doing all those exercises, why am I feeling attracted towards Shefali". I have interacted with many women, but I never got this feeling; I don't know what it is." . He loves Trisha, but he is too attracted to Shefali. I have to control these feelings. Vasant, in confusion, calls Trisha, and when Trisha picks up the call, Vasant wants to tell her what he feels about Shefali, but in his fear, he just wraps up his thoughts and says, "So you are working on yourself", Trisha hasn't worked on her diet, and she doesn't focus much on it. So she says, "I will do it whenever I want." . In that moment, Vasant became so angry and said "So you are not doing it on a regular basis, and I think you are following a good diet also". Trisha, in aggression, said, "Well, I will not lie, but I can't eat grass all the time; it is so hard, and what if I will not change? Do you leave me?" Vasant replied, "Of course not, but......", Trisha said,"There is no if and but," and after that, Vasant cut the call. Now this time this small talk has taken the form of a big issue, and this time Vasant gets very exhausted and thinks she doesn't have to behave. Like that. He felt hurt, and the sensitivity in his heart increased because he felt that it was all like discouragement towards his choices. He lost his mind, and then overwhelming thoughts covered Vasant's whole mind. And whenever he feels lost, he calls her friend, Shefali. When Shefali received the phone call and said "Hello Vasant, so how do you remember me today?", Vasant replied, "Shefali, there is nothing like that, you know, but actually today my girlfriend has put so many arguments on me, and that makes me so frown, and now my mind is bursting". Shefali calmed him down and said, "Can you tell me what is the problem?" . Vasant said, "Well, leave it, so how are you doing right now?" Shefali replied, "Well, I am good. If you are not feeling well, we can go outside". Vasant said, "Yeah, why not? It will be a refreshing break for me, so where are we going?", Shefali said. "Well, we can go to the nearest Galleria Fountain Park. It can be calming for you". Shefali's inner feminine really wants to impress him, so he decided to wear something keen and serene so that he gets impressed. After that, Shefali reached the flat of Vasant, and then she made a phone call to Vasant. Vasant picked up her call and said "Hey, where are you?", Shefali said, "I am at the gate of your flat. Can you come to pick me up?" Vasant assured on the call and said "Yeah, I am coming downstairs", Vasant ran on the stairs and opened the door, where he saw Shefali standing in a beautiful pink embroidery kurti with beautiful jhumkas, and then Vasant recited, "Woah!! You look good in traditional clothes." Shefali replied "Yeah, of course I am a model; I have to look great in every outfit". Shefali said "Okay, now sit on the backseat and let me take you to a wonderful park to give you a view of beautiful flowers and greenery that would make you feel more relaxed and enhanced". Vasant sat in the backseat, and Shefali started driving. With a crazy ride, they reach "the beautiful parks of Fenora,", which are full of flowers and just look like a small valley of charismatic meadows. Shefali started talking, and they sat on the park bench. Vasant said Shefali, what would you like to eat?", Shefali looked over the items and said Vasant, just bring me a packet of popcorn and nothing else". Vasant said "Just popcorn". Shefali nodded her head, and then Vasant came with two packets of popcorn. He gave one packet to Shefali, sat down on the bench, and said "I felt you were a very mature woman". How did you become such a responsible person?" Shefali replied "Of course everything comes with experiences, and I come up from bad experiences, and all those things make me feel that I have to live on my own and not be very dependent on anyone". Vasant replied, "You know you are mature, but Trisha is very childish. I like her for each and every quality of being childish, but at some points everyone needs to mature, and she shows a lack of interest in everything I ask. I ask her to maintain her physique; she doesn't; I ask her to focus on goals; she doesn't; and she repeatedly asks me to give her more time. Sefali I am the eldest son of my family, and I have so many responsibilities to set up my career. I can't bring her that dreamy life that she has imagined, and for that life right now, I have to focus". Shefali said "Well, in that case, you have to throw the responsibility on her so that she can recognise them and start transforming". Vasant said Well, I don't want to pressurise her to work and do everything, so I don't say anything to her, but now I think I have to do something, but I don't have any idea how to do it or what to do, but surely I will find some responsibility for her". Shefali replied, "Let her take the time, and I think this time when you go back home, go and meet her. Why don't you join the tuition again for weekends so that you will meet her in the same way you previously did, and that's how, with work, you both can meet". Vasant said "As a woman you are advising, I hope it makes things good between us". By listening to all of this, Shefali can control her attraction towards him and give advice based on facts about women, but somewhere she is sure that if Vasant gives her a chance, she will surely grab it. But she says everything in favour of Trisha because she wants to gain her trust. Vasant had established herself as an honest and decent person through that conversation. after a great conversation and when Vasant felt calmness in that Valley. He has decided to make better efforts for Trisha. Shefali again asked, "Does she have a problem with our friendship?". Vasant replied "Why?". Shefali said "Maybe sometimes when our partner spends more time with another person, our partner may feel insecure", Vasant said, "Yeah, maybe it can be a reason; she is so frustated, and may be that can be the reason of every argument. Okay, I have to make her realise that when this weekend I go back home, I will surely talk to her and clear everything out". Vasant said, "I think you are getting late and you have to go home alone, so let's go back. Your safety is my priority". Shefali smiled and said, Okay," and then they drove back home.

Now, slowly, weekdays are ending and weekends have started. On Friday, Vasant took a bus and started his journey to home. where he messaged Trisha, "I am coming. , after returning from tuition, saw the notification on her phone, and when she opened her phone, she found the message from Vasant. She was upset with Vasant, but when she read that Vasant was coming back home, she got full of enthusiasm and energy. She quickly called Vasant to ask about the status of his journey. where Vasant picked up her call and said, "Hey, my love, are you happy now? Last week, I found you so upset, so I have decided to come for you". Trisha replied "Where have you reached?". Vasant replied "Ah, well, I don't know the exact location, but it will take three hours to reach home". So Trisha said "Okay, come to meet me after tuition". Vasant said, "Of course, when you come out of the door of Mrs. Yashika's house, I will be there standing for you. Trisha was so happy with that fact, and she fell asleep with dreams of meeting him after a long time.

The next day, she wakes up with a smile and goes to class. After that, with calmness, she comes back home. Now, happily, she gets ready with a green kurti and white leggings; in contrast, she wore those jhumkas that Vasant had gifted to her. She makes her look good, and then, after attending tuition, she comes out with excitement from the house of Mrs. Yashika and starts imagining him. She is walking calmly in her womanhood and talking every step so elegantly, but she saw Vasant nowhere; she was looking here and there in his search, and suddenly the echoed voice reached in the ear of Trisha, where she turned and saw Vasant standing on the edge of the road with a pink rose in his hand, and Trisha excitedly ran towards him and hugged him publicly. Vasant also gave her a hug, and after that, he said, Trisha, we are in a public area, but it's okay, let's go". They started walking together, and then Vasant took her to a restaurant and said, "Trisha, I want to say something. Trisha said "okay". They are now walking still because Trisha is getting into suspense because she has no idea what he is going to say, and now they are sitting in one corner, where Vasant asks her to order, so Trisha, by her choice, orders some food items. After that, they both calmed down. Now Trisha is a little nervous, but she said, "Okay, Vasant, don't leave me in suspense and tell whatever you want to say; bad thoughts are covering my whole mind."

Vasant realised that Trisha's insecurity was the root cause of their arguments. He understood that he needed to reassure Trisha of his love and commitment to her. He took a deep breathe, held Trisha's hands, and said, "Trisha, I love you, and you are the only one in my life. Shefali is just a friend, and there is nothing more than that. You are the one I want to spend my life with." Trisha's eyes filled with tears, and she felt a wave of relief wash over her. She knew that Vasant was sincere and that he loved her.

Vasant continued, "Trisha, I understand that you feel left out, and I promise that I will make more time for you. I don't want you to feel insecure or jealous. I will do whatever it takes to make you feel loved and wanted." Trisha's heart filled with warmth, and she felt grateful to have a partner who loved her so much.

They both hugged each other, and Trisha whispered, "I love you too, Vasant. I don't want to lose you." Vasant kissed her forehead and said, "You will never lose me, Trisha. I am yours forever." They both smiled, and their love became stronger than ever. After that, when he drops Trisha back home, he makes all the plans for her, and this time when he returns home, Trisha comes to meet her at the bus stop. Somehow, right now, the situation settles down.

From that day on, Vasant made more time for Trisha, and they spent quality time together. He also made it a point to include her in his conversations with Shefali, and Trisha felt more included and less left out. She started to trust Vasant again, and their love grew deeper. They both realised that love is not just about being with each other; it is also about understanding each other's insecurities and working towards overcoming them together.

Trisha also started to get to know her. She realised that Shefali was not a threat to their relationship but a good friend who brought positivity into their lives. Vasant and Trisha's relationship grew stronger than ever, and they both knew that they could overcome any challenge that came their way. Now everything is going at a good pace, and everything is alright. Vasant is now too happy with the changes he found in Trisha, and that all happens when Trisha becomes sure that Shefali is just a friend, so Vasant thought that she would meet Shefali this weekend to say thanks.

When the weekend started, Vasant called Shefali to meet, and they met in a cafe with coffee and started talking. So Vasant said, "Thank you, Shefali; you have helped me so much. You know, this time she is so happy, and I feel like she is more comfortable and focused. You have told me the route problem, and when you have solved that and cleared that out, now she is so happy, and now we don't have arguments". Where Shefali said, Oh, it's my responsibility to help you, Vasant, because I am a woman too", she continued and said, Well, Vasant, are you interested in going out on a trip to the mountains? It is not too far; we can easily reach there and enjoy it. Where Vasant said, Oh, I will ask Nishad and Trisha for thaa trip. Although Shefali didn't like the idea of going there altogether, she still said, Yeah, okay. So Vasant made a call to Trisha for this plan, and Trisha, on the first call, didn't pick up the phone. Then Vasant said, "Well, she is not picking up my phone; maybe she is busy. Okay, now let me ask Nishad". Vasant called Nishad, and he picked up the call and said "Hello Brother, what is going on", Vasant directly asked him Nishad asked, Nishad, do you want to go out for a trip?", Nishad quickly replied, No, no! Brother, I am going out for a week to my home because my father has called me for a week", Vasant said "Oh well, it's okay, brother". After Nishad cut the call, suddenly Trisha's call started coming on Vasant's phone. Vasant quickly picked up the call and said "Hello, my love", Trisha replied "So how is everything going?", Vasant said "Well, I am going out with my friends on a trip, and I also want to take you to that trip; do you come with us?", Trisha's mind went on a frission, and she replied, "Have you not been aware of my mother's anger issues? If I am outside for more than two days, she starts creating drama.but I can try to join you, Vasant". he realises and says, "Yeah, I know your mother is very strict. Okay, well, I really want you to go with us". Trisha in sad affirmative face said "us? , well how many friends are going with you?", so Vasant knew that if he tells that he will be going with Shefali Trisha destroy his plan and get jealous again, so Vasant lie to Trisha and said "Nishad and some other classmates", Trisha said "oh okay well enjoy, cause I am going press some clothes, I will call you an hour later", Vasant replied "okay my love, bye". and the conversation between Vasant and Trisha has ended. Now Vasant put the phone on the table, went back and sat on the chair, and started talking to Shefali and said, "Well Nishad and Trisha may be go with us. there are less chances of them, if they didn't go so we two have to go for more than one day trip". After hearing that, Shefali became super excited, and somehow she started calculating all the evaluation, and said, Vasant, so we go out for tomorrow, so pack your bag", Vasant said "Yeah, and we will go to Sweet Talk Mountains, okay", Shefali said

"I didn't get it, Vasant" and Vasant said "how you don't know about that beautiful, serene place?", Shefali replied, "Well, I don't know anything about this place, but okay, done," and then Shefali dropped Vasant over his flat went back to her home. at night when Vasant was talking with Trisha and he ask again for the trip, so Trisha said "Vasant I talk to my mother and ask her for permission, by telling her that I am going with Swati, but still Anubhav knows about you, so he already have a idea, and he refused", Vasant said "I really want to take you to those hills, but it's fine" and her plan got cancelled .

Next morning at 7 a.m., Shefali called Vasant and said "Are you ready?", Vasant said "Yeah, I am coming". Vasant takes her bag and gets out, and when he saw Shefali in that skinny V-shaped top and hot pants, Vasant's heartbeat raised up, and he said Wow, Shefali, you are looking glamorous as always", Shefali passed a smile, and she said, Yeah, thank you so much. Well, I don't know about Sweet Talker Mountains, so I am driving till Song River, and then after that, you will lead us.....okay". Vasant replied, "Okay," and sat on the backseat. Shefali started driving the scooter, and the beautiful journey of roads has started, where all the buildings and trees are starting to construct that journey that is slowly going to turn into nostalgia. Slowly, each tree passes by the heart of Vasant, and because Vasant was going out only with Shefali, strange thoughts of Shefali have started covering the whole mind of Vasant, and her eyes always lead him to her. Shefali, whose inner urge wants him to see her, has been completing it because she has a crush on her, and when from the mirror Shefali observes that from hidden eyes Vasant was trying to look at her heartbeat, it also starts raising. Somehow, somewhere, they started feeling attracted towards eachother. Vasant thought it was a natural process because he was sitting with a girl, so attraction towards her was usual, but Shefali was taking it in other terms because she had a crush on him, so she lent into so many feelings. Those feelings form a stack and bind her heart and mind. Now she wants to feel that closure, but the situation was different. So slowly, as they passed each trees, the things between them started getting deeper, and now Shefali has decided that she will win Vasant's heart with her selfless efforts, her personality, and her status to get what she wants with the carrot and the stick. Now after a few hours of driving, they both get hungry and stop for a Maggi point, and then Vasant started ordered food, and he said Brother, two plates of Maggi and two teas", where Shefali said," order one plate of Maggi only because I am not too hungry right now; there is no requirement for two plates; I will eat with you only". Vasant doubt and thought of her clinginess towards him, but showcased everything like he didn't get it. They brought one plate of maggi and two teas, and when they started eating that amazing vegetable masala maggi, it tasted so delicious, especially because they were going into clouds. So it's making them feel delighted now that Vasant has taken one sip of tea and Shefali has taken the same sip from the same cup, and that's creating a little awkwardness, but then she said " Oh, sorry, I was mistaken with your cup". After that, Vasant stops doubting her clinginess a little, and They complete their meal. Shefali said, "Vasant, now you should drive to Sweet Talkers Mountain because now I am feeling tired. Vasant said, "Yeah, sit, let me make you feel thrill," and Vasant started clenching, and then Shefali sat on the backseat, and then Vasant started driving, and then he put his hand on the accelerator and increased the speed, and Shefali loved that because she loved doing adventurous stuff, and in excitement, she unheld her hands and opened them to touch the high speed winds, and she blew out her voice with her highest note; it was so shrill that it sounds like whistling saprano. At the same moment, they are passing through a tunnel, so a strange echoed voice comes out that sounds a little scary. They both Heard and after realisation, that it's their own echo, they laughed over that sound, and Vasant slowed down the bike and said, "How was that, Shefali?" Shefali replied "Well, that was fabulous; my heart comes out in my hand, but all over it feels so breathtaking, and then Vasant replied Okay, but now I am driving slowly, because now roads are getting a little narrow on mountains, and I can't take a risk now". Shefali made a dumb face, and then she said "Okay, Vasant". On a medium pace, they started covering mountains, where, after riding up for a few miles, suddenly a noise sounded into the ears of Vasant and Shefali, so they stopped their scooter, and then Vasant said: "Well, what is this?, It's sounding very strange; do you have any idea about that?", Shefali also refused and said, "No, I didn't", but then their sight falls on a local shop, which is a small sweet shop, where in the big jars there are different sweets like besan Ladoo (gramflour), motichoor ladoo, tarmind with powedered sugar, and other sweets were placed. Vasant and Shefali felt the appetite for those sweets, and Vasant said, "Brother, please pack six ladoos; Shefali, what would you like to eat?", Shefali said Well, I love besan ladoos, so pack half kg for me; I will then take it for my mom", Vasant asked the shopkeeper, "Brother, how much?" and he replied "Two fifty rupees, sir", Vasant took out his Wallet and take out a note of two hundred and one note of fifty and give it to them and said "brother what is this strange sound, Is there is any Traditional function going on there?", so Shopkeeper tells "bhaiya near to our Village there is a monk, where they are celebrating their cultural fair, so they are performing their cultural event and from there this typical music sound is coming". With the sound of bells, drums and trumpet were rasing Shefali's enthusiasm, and she said, Vasant, I think we have to go there to join the fair", Vasant said, " Why not, Shefali? That is so interesting to reach out to different cultural things. Well, it is so fascinating for me, Shefali, to know about diversity in culture and places, let's go". So Vasant and Trisha started their scooter and stop there, and there they found big green entrance door that is fully open. When Shefali and Vasant enter the fair, the crowd is sitting in a circle, and in the centre there are people dressed up in colourful clothes and jewellery that Vasant and Shefali are not familiar with. but still, their cultural dress impressed both of them. They started their traditional dance where the whole serene place was covered with a lovely crowd and the melody of bells and their choir, where those tebitian dresses and several colours were mixing in their eyes. Vasant said to Shefali " Wow, this place is vibing so cool". Shefali replied, "Yeah, I also like this. Vasant, have you seen the things that they are selling in the outside market? Let's go. I like few things that I would like to buy". So they went out from there and went to those street shops where beautiful Tebitian monk-related stones and bells were selling. Also, different styles of clothes are on sale, and Shefali likes all of them. So she said "I want to buy at least a dress from this market". where she viewed different shops and chose a store where; a girl of her age was sitting and selling clothes. So Shefali and Vasant went into the store, and Shefali said to that girl, "Hey, your collection is so cool. I just like it. Is there a trial room?", So that shopkeeper girl said, "Thank you, mam. Well, yeah, see, our trial room is here in the right corner.". Shefali picked up a pink dress and went to the trial room. When she wore that dress, she found it to be so pretty and goreous on her, and in one go, she decided to buy that dress. She came out of the trial room and started asking the price, saying, "Hey, how much does that cost?", to which the shopkeeper girl replied, Mam, it is for one thousand and seven fifty". Shefali finds it impressive, and the price is also fine, so she brought that dress.Vasant said "That's good, Shefali; you don't take too much time in selecting the dresses", Shefali smiled and said "At least you like me for a single thing". Vasant found these words to be very sarcastic, and the expression on her face was intensely confusing. In that, Vasant said, "Alright, let's go, cause it's getting too late, because we stopped for the fair and we didn't reach the sweettalkers mountains. Shefali said "Vasant, listen, we are not running in a race; that we have to reach there at any cost by today; take a slow pace; enjoy; and then wherever you reach, that will be our destination, okay". Previously, what she said sounded a little sarcastic, but Vasant found these words to be very honest that came from her mouth. Vasant has started liking her vibe now, even her thought process. After that, Vasant started driving for Sweet Talkers Hills, and in between that journey, something inside Vasant has changed, and now everything is too comforting for Vasant, and they are talking and enjoying the ride, because now in reaching those long roads, Vasant feels an attachment with her, the same attachment that Shefali was also feeling, so slowly the area that was reserved for Trisha is now allocated to Shefali, and there in his heart,in his mind, every closet is filled with the notions of Shefali. Destiny also stands on Shefali's side, and the weather changed there in the mountains. Now it started raining heavily. Vasant said, "Shefali I guess weather is not good for driving, because now 'landslides' and 'clouds breaking' are very common here, so maybe it creates some problems for us." Shefali found these words so surreal due to her passionate and stubborn thoughts. Shefali went to her thoughts because, at that moment, God was in her favour, and the drops of water that were hailing with rain, didn't want to stop, and that made her gut feel like this was an opportunity for Shefali to make him hers. And she said, "Yeah, okay, see those cottages; you didn't know Vasant, but this looks so similar to my dream cottage that I have seen and imagined". Vasant again saw spark in her eyes that he likes. Vasant said: "oh really, I am so lucky enough, that I am randomly helping you to persue your this vintage cottage dream". Shefali repiled "yeah, It may be a little more costly, but I believe in making my dreams come true because I am a stubborn person as you know" . In happiness, everything is leading him towards her, so he is kind of happy, because he got the chance, and he said, "Okay, so let's go! and they ran towards those cottages where they went into reception hall and where, in the formal white shirt, in black coat, and in black pants, a big fatty receptionist was standing. Vasant with Shefali went inside, where receptionist said "Welcome sir and mam to our cottages, how can I help you?", Vasant asked, "We want to book, umm, wait". He turned towards Shefali and said "Two rooms? , right!!" Shefali said, "What will we do for two rooms? We are here to enjoy", Vasant replied "Well, you are a girl, and it is my responsibility to make you feel safe, and I just thought to ask you first, but you don't have any problems, so okay, that's so great". The receptionist asks, Sir, can you provide your identification proof because these mountains and curly roads are full of creatures, so we require them". Vasant found his words a little jumbled, which he didn't understand too well, but he said "okay". He turned towards Shefali to take her ID, and she said "Oh, I forgot all my IDs. Well, is it a softcopy that's allowed", So the receptionist said "Yeah, sure mam", so Shefali said "Okay, I am sending you over email, so provide me your email ID." Where receptionist show her the board on which email Ids were mentioned,". Trisha sent him the id proof online, and when he received it, he asked a supporting staff member to take their luggage and show them the assigned cottage, and when they reached that cottage, When they go inside the cottage, a beautiful dreamy vintage aura runs into their brain, they was so good to feel. even all the wooden architecture was startling. After that, the supporting staff, who is a guy of Vasant and Shefali's age and a native of the mountains, said "If you need something, call me for assistance at the given telephone number", and Vasant said "Okay......thanks!!". and they went inside, and now Shefali and Vasant started discussing this beautiful cottage, and Vasant said "I have seen beautiful cottages like this only in movies", Shefali agreed with Vasant and said, "Same with me, because I usually went to hotels, but never into a big wooden exquisite cottage like this.

Nestled amidst a picturesque landscape, the green and white wooden hill cottage exudes charm and tranquilly. Surrounded by lush greenery, this quaint retreat stands proudly atop a gentle slope, providing a breathtaking view of the rolling hills that stretch as far as the eye can see.

The cottage itself was the harmonious blend of rustic elegance and idyllic simplicity. The exterior, painted in a soothing shade of white, showcases the craftsmanship of the wooden panels that form the walls. The choice of white highlights the cottage's natural beauty while also reflecting the soft sunlight that bathes the area, creating a serene ambiance.Accentuating the cottage's enchanting appeal, a variety of vibrant green vines, ivy, and climbing roses adorn the exterior walls, entwining themselves around the wooden beams and windows. These natural embellishments bring life to the cottage, adding a touch of whimsy and a connection to the surrounding nature.The hilly cottage features a steep roof covered in moss, giving it an enchanting, fairytale-like charm. The wooden shingles, weathered by time, provide an authentic and rustic touch to the cottage's overall aesthetic.

As you step inside, you are greeted by a warm and inviting interior. The living area is cosy and features exposed wooden beams on the ceiling, looks simply great. The walls are painted in a soothing shade of green, complementing the surrounding as pretty as a picture.Plush cushions in shades of green and white offer comfort and invite relaxation. Large windows allow ample natural light to fill the room of Vasant and shefali, This evening feels so special cause it rainy.The cottage includes a small, well-equipped kitchen, that too much adored by Shefali and a charming dining area where one can enjoy meals while gazing out at the picturesque landscape, where Vasant sit and started gasping. A winding wooden staircase leads to a cosy bedroom on the upper floor, featuring a comfortable bed adorned with soft white linens. From here, one can wake up to the stunning panoramic views that unfold beyond the windows.

Surrounded by nature's tranquility, the green and white wooden hilly cottage offers an escape from the bustling world to Vasant. Cause with time the responsibility and anxiety for life has raised where that place was comforting him. Vasant and Shefali sit miles away from people, life, and stress. after analysing the whole cottage they went in the main room and Shefali removed her wet socks, and she said, "Well,our clothes are a little wet, so, Vasant, we need to change our clothes. I am going to change my clothes. You also need to change your clothes; otherwise, you catch a cough or illness". Vasant felt very shy and awkward, but he said, "okay; You change here, and I am going to change in the hall. After some time, he knocked on the door, so Shefali opened her door, and Vasant saw his shy mode get on. Vasant's gaze fell upon Shefali, who stood before him in a delicately adorned camisole and Bermuda shorts. In that fleeting moment, an undeniable spark ignited between them—a magnetic force that transcended mere attraction. Vasant was captivated by Shefali's beauty, her confident demeanour, and the alluring way she carried herself. A surge of desire coursed through his veins—a deep longing to know her more intimately. The connection they shared was electric, a dance of unspoken desires that hinted at a profound connection beyond the physical realm. Their eyes locked, silently conveying a mutual yearning that went beyond the realms of everyday encounters. It was a meeting of souls—a tantalising glimpse into a world where passion and fascination intertwined. Since then, everything between Vasant and Shefali has changed. Now all the things and places in his heart that Vasant has dedicated to Trisha were changed because Vasant has started feeling comfortable with Shefali in a way he never felt comfortable with Trisha. He never found Trisha to be an understanding person; that cottage became the memory of their beginning. They started discussing things. Vasant asked Shefali, Did you have those feelings for me previously or did whatever happened between us just suddenly?", Shefali replied, "Well, I like you since I have seen you in the tuition, but because you are already dating Trisha, I never get a chance to say that I really like you, and now it feels like that I love you! What about you?", Vasant replied. See, honestly, if I tell you, I love Trisha a lot, but I never found her mature and understanding. I have asked her only one thing: to take care of her health and to reduce her weight and just to maintain her, but she always blames me for that and says that you have to love me the way I am. I can accept that, but many times I don't feel comfortable because we don't look compatible with each other." When I saw you in the classroom, all my insecurities awakened, and Then I felt attacked, but I opposed my thoughts. Now that I came out of that small town and I come to know more about life, I felt free from her. With you, it felt so easy that I never felt it with her because she always looked for attention. But then I just balanced the things. Now I am feeling so much for you, and I didn't want to go back to her after all I have great memories with you and I am know sure enough that you love me. Now going back to her feels like a prison to me. So now I also think that I love you!", So Shefali asked, "how will you detach from Trisha?, because I always saw that she is a very clingy person. I know, as a good person, you are just dealing with your mess, but you know you don't need to. It is not necessary to make everyone feel comfortable; do what you feel and what you love." Vasant said "Now I have decided to come out of her toxic relationship, and I have to ask her for a breakup". Shefali agrees with Vasant's decision. At night, they give a call to the assigned telephone number and order a good, delicious meal. They eat together, talk with each other, and then fall asleep.

The next day, they decided to continue to the Sweet Talkers Mountains. They packed up their luggage and checked out of that cottage. Then the supporting staff left their small luggage bag on their scooter, and they slowly started driving the scooter up hills, where the curvy hills and narrow roads made their journey a little rough. Rough is tough, but it gaves a feel of thrill to them. That is what Shefali and Vasant were feeling, and now they are sitting in a way that makes them look like they are stuck together. They are enjoying their journey like lovers on the road, which had started a day before. The whole valley is full of flowers and butterflies. This place is looking like a sweet meadow that no one has ever imagined or seen. and they finally reach those sweet talkers hills, where people are camping. They roam all around the hills, and Hydragea candybelle is all over there on the road. With the sound of wind and the aroma of flowers, the whole valley looks like heaven to them. While strolling through the quaint street, Shefali and Vasant stumbled upon a beautiful church nestled among the surrounding forest flowers and traditional street food cafes. Shefali's eyes got stuck on that church because she had never been to a church, and she thought that by going there, she could fulfil her dream of also being in the church with a lover. She seemed very desperate to have been in that church. Vasant saw her love for church, so he said, Shefali, let's go; we are going into this church", He turned back, reversed his bike towards church, and parked the scooter aside. Vasant said "Let me check if it is open or not", So one Priest is standing near the park around the church, and Vasant asks from outside, Father, can we come inside?", to which the priest replies, "Yes, it is open, my child. The church is hidden under a canopy of lush green pine trees, where the walls of yellow contrast with white and the red roofs give it beautiful asthetics, and where, with the help of stones, they are giving it an ancient look. Curiosity filled their hearts as they pushed open the brown, heavy wooden doors, revealing a sight that left them in awe. The interior was adorned with intricate stained glass windows, which Shefali first saw from inside. When they entered, they started feeling a pure vibe that Shefali found to be very devotional. It seems like the church has something that makes them pure. Shefali asked Vasant "Are you also feeling something pure and vibrant inside your soul?", Vasant replied Yes, I can also feel those vibes; it is serene and beautiful to feel like that", They both went near the candle stand, where they lit their candles for their faith. Hand in hand, they wandered through the hallowed space, marvelling at the architectural marvels and the sense of history that permeated every corner. It was an unexpected detour that allowed them to immerse themselves in the beauty and spirituality of the moment, creating a memory that would forever remain etched in their hearts. They stand in front of Jesus, and they both confess everything to him. After that, Shefali saw books in one corner, and where she saw the Bible, she started turning the pages to get an idea of where Vasant was sitting so calmly on the bench. they don't really wants to get out of it, but then Vasant said "Shefali I think we have spent enough time here, so know let's go", Shefali said "yeah I know, Okay let's go".they go back sit over on the scooty and then they went to street cafe and fill their empty stomachs and now slowly cause the day is ending and they have to reach back, so Vasant said "okay Shefali now we have to go back, cause tommorow we have to go back to our schedules, ahh we have to end this trip now, that is so sad", Shefali said "yeah I am going to miss you, so can I know Vasant, what is in your mind for me?",Vasant replied "Shefali, I went to church with holding your hand, you don't get what it means?", Shefali said "even if I know everything still, i want to hear it from you", where Vasant said "I wants to make you mine at I am breaking up with Trisha, and I really want to say, I love you". Shefali said, "I love you too! and they hugged each other, and then with a smile, Shefali said Vasant, now get up, Vasant laughed and said "You have something that attracts me towards you; your everything, even your figure; all things are so perfect", Shefali replied, "I know I am hot! With laughs, they went out and sat on the scooty, and they reached back home, where he dropped Shefali at her flat and went back to his flat, and the journey ended. this is how: EVERYTHING HAS CHANGED!!.

EVERYTHING HAS CHANGED

Everything suddenly changed between Trisha and Vasant, but, everything changing can't change the feelings restored in the heart's repository. Trisha still has a beating heart for him. Vasant still has respect in his heart for Trisha, but there is a drop of love left; it seems like there is no place left for love. The whole thing is covered by the beauty of Shefali. In the fight between beauty and love, beauty wins, and this is something so common because we are unable to absorb and notice the hidden things; we believe in what we see. It is just like we love flowers because they are beautiful and we can see them, but we don't love for those green leaves because they make the flowers look more beautiful in their greenery, but you can't choose them over flowers.

Now that Vasant had started loving Someone else, so he started ignoring Trisha's calls. Trisha, on the other side, hasn't called him again and again. She didn't have any idea what would happen to him. She thought he might be busy with work, due to which, he is not picking up the phone. but as the days increase, there is no call back from Vasant's side. Trisha now gets scared and starts thinking, "Is he fine? Where is he? Is Vasant safe? He is even not picking up my call from last week. Anyway, I have to check. Okay, so let's find out Nishad's phone number. He is my only hope now", Now she was so conscious of him that she starts calling him again and again. After ignoring too many calls, Vasant got irritated with her calling pattern, and he picked up the call and said with a shouting voice, "Hello, why are you disturbing me again and again? I am very busy nowadays, but your small stupid head didn't understand it right", Trisha murmured. "You are not picking up my call from the last week, and my heart is very upset. What can I do about that", Vasant replied, "Okay, now you can see I am alright, so can you please cut the call? I will talk with you later", Trisha's heart got sober by the cruel words of Vasant, and she felt embarassed, but she didn't cut the call because her love and innocence didn't allow her, and at that time Vasant said Trisha " don't cry, please; I didn't want to make you cry; okay, I am not cutting the call; let's talk", and suddenly the smile on the face of Trisha came back and she said "I am missing you so badly and you are talking like that, you even didn't want to tallk even thougn a week hen passed, didn't you miss me?", Vasant replied "I am stuck in something, just not in a mood actually to talk that is why I have talked so rudely, but I am sorry for that. Trisha felt so calm from inside by those words, and with a happy heart, she said "Okay, if you didn't like to talk to me yet, so call me after sometime when you are feeling fine", Vasant felt like an ungrateful guy, and he said "Okay.". With all that, his brain opposing Trisha anyhow. Vasant felt very uncomfortable because she made him feel like she was playing the victim card in front of him , which is why she started crying like a sober baby. With that mindset, his thought process for Trisha has changed, and he realises that he has never been interested in her. First, she shows her up like an innocent girl and wins his heart, and now, after a year, he realises that he is not into him, so he doesn't like to talk to her, but by showing her tears and fears, her insecurity, she again gains all the sympathy and keeps stuck with me, and now he is unable to feel that love for her. The second thing that comes out is her body physique and personality, which he never finds attractive, and whenever he asks about change, she always refuses instead of choosing to workout. He knew why he was leaving her, because getting attracted to someone else was the only reason.

These all things together make her incompatible for him, and now he is sure that leaving her is not a bad decision. If two people aren't feeling happy together, the relationship feels like a burden, and that is Vasant's thought process and situation. He is feeling like he is in a swamp with her. He tried a lot to protect him from getting attracted to someone else, but the way Shefali cames into his life makes him feel that he is in a relationship but not happy within it. So now he criticises all the good things about Trisha and just looks at her weaknesses, and when you start looking at someone's weak points, you automatically underestimate his image and start making judgements on that basis, no matter how great that person actually is. This is where Vasant has stuck.

When Shefali gets free from her schedule, she feels a frisson on her lips, and she looks towards her memories of the trip and feels so calm and soft in her imagination. Those cloudy, dreamy thoughts of Adreline harmone are almost equivalent to a drug. Both Shefali and Trisha are dreaming the same, but their intensity of love varies. Now Vasant is free from his mind, and he has decided to call Shefali. He put everything aside and started talking with Sefali. When Shefali saw the call from Vasant, she pray into happiness and said, Vasant, I was waiting for your call. Vasant said "Yeah, I am also missing you, so I just folded all my work to call you", In excitement, Shefali said "I am reimagining every memory that I have made with you". They slowly started talking about more and more things. Then Vasant said, "Shefali, you already know that my girlfriend is Trisha, but now I am going to break up with her for you. Before that, I want to ask about your past because I want to know everything about you. I don't want any secrets between us", Shefali replied" No, Vasant, I never had any relationship with anyone" and after that talk, Vasant said "That is so great, Shefali; I am very happy after listening to this". Within those talks and pauses, they loved each other. Vasant continued that candy talk. Vasant said "Thank you, Shefali, for coming into my life; otherwise, I have to adjust with Trisha". Shefali laughed and said, "Well, okay, Vasant, it is getting late; I have a work schedule for tomorrow." Vasant said, "Okay, sweetheart, good night" . After that talk, Vasant felt so good that he is now comfortable with her. Now he feels so compatible and better than he ever felt with Trisha.

Now each and every day, Shefali and Vasant started talking. For giving time to her, she cuts the time of Trisha. Another week passed with Vasant ignoring Trisha. Now Trisha started feeling overwhelmed and sober with that, and now she decided to find the contact number of Nishad, so she called Swati, and Swati picked up the call of Trisha and said "Hello Trisha, how are you", So Trisha replied "I am fine, Swati; I am in a hurry; can you please search out the number of Nishad for me". Swati got worried and said, "What happened, Trisha? Please tell me". Trisha replied, Swati, I will tell you everything later. First, search out the contact number of Nishad". Swati replied, "Okay, I will message you," and after five minutes of searching, Swati found out the contact information of Nishad, then she messaged Trisha. When Trisha got her number, he picked up the call and said "Hello, Trisha, so you have called me for Vasant?". where Trisha replied "Yeah, he is picking up my call; you are his roommate; can you tell me the problem and why he is doing so", So Nishad replied sarcastically, "You should know about this, and you are asking me!"", Trisha gets angry, but she controls her anger and says, "Okay, please give him the phone. I want to talk to him". Nishad replied, "Oh, I am so sorry, but he is not here; when he comes back, I will let you know". When Trisha come to knew that, she gets the clear idea that he is out with someone else and that there must be something suspicious about Vasant that they are hiding. Trisha really got worried and didn't have any idea what to do now; she was just waiting for the call. Her sober face is telling a deep story of being scared. To get out of this situation, Trisha thought to share her feelings and emotions with Swati, so she made a phone call to her, and after two rings, Swati took the call and said, "Hey Trisha, how are you? Is everything fine?", Trisha, in a sober voice, replied to her, Swati, there is a lot I have been going through. You know, Vasant hasn't taken my calls since last week, and every time he just says to me that he is busy with some work, he doesn't give me two minutes to talk. I can feel there is something suspicious going on; there is something that Vasant is hiding from me. If there is any problem together, we can easily solve it, but now he doesn't even give me any opportunity to make things better; instead, he believes in ignoring my calls. I didn't have any idea why this was happening to me", Swati, when she heard this in a sober tone, understood that she was suffering because of him, so She said, "Don't be sad; I will help you. It is so bad of him whenever he calls back. Don't start talking like a despo again. Just make him first clear out what is going on, and after that only, talk with him about unnecessarily complicated things. I will try to help you by finding out with the help of Nishad", Trisha said "But I also talked to him, but he didn't tell me anything; he just said that it's your matter and you should know about this". Swati said, "You are too innocent for this. Don't worry, I am trying", Trisha said "Thank you for always being there for me", Swati said, "Oh, Trisha, these words are needless; you are like my soul sister," and she cuts the call, where Swati, with the help of her other friends, tries to put pressure on the head of Nishad to tell him what is going on. but Nishad is not telling anything, but when a lot of friends start asking, he calls Vasant. Where Vasant is with Shefali, he takes the call and says, "What happened, Nishad? Why are you calling me this time, when I am on an outing", Nishad tells him "Everyone is asking me about you; what should I tell everyone?", Vasant says, Nishad, don't worry, today I will call her and make her clear out everything", Nishad says, "Okay brother, best of luck!" and he cuts the call. After spending time with Shefali, Vasant went back to his place to complete the daily tasks and his work priorities.

After that, with a heavy heart, he decided to call Trisha, but it is really tough to say goodbye to someone. It is even getting harder for him to tell her because it is sounding cruel to Vasant, but he has already taken the decision to choose his girl, and he has chosen Shefali for him. Goodbye is a sorrow that pretends and makes us feel like everything is just going to end without even ending the paths on which the soul has once walked. It didn't end, but there was just a change in direction. Goodbyes are so sad; that feels like a curse to the soul. Now Vasant is also standing on the edge of saying goodbye, but he is very clear of his commitments,and because he doesn't love her anymore, saying goodbye should be easy, but that is not the same situation with Trisha. Her innocence and kindness were never able to make her run away, even in this situation. She makes the beliefs, and she wants to live those beliefs. Where her one promise and belief was "to keep loving your lover till the end", that belief bound her to love him, take care of him, and keep loving him anyhow. Now Vasant took the mobile phone in his hand and opened the dial list to call Trisha. He opened the contact, but he was not able to press the call button. He felt so rude and scared that he must be doing something wrong, because somewhere he knows that he likes Shefali because she is beautiful. Shefali didn't love her the way Trisha does, which made him feel so scared that he might regret his decision. In his messy mind, he got tangled and sat down on the bed because he was exhausted.

Now some of their old friends from school have taken admission to the same place where Vasant was living. When they were out, they noticed Shefali and Vasant. So slowly the rumour spreads because that thing started passing from one person to another, and that's how it also reaches the ears of Swati, and when she comes to know that fact, she feels very sorry for Trisha. She is now going to tell Trisha this. Her facial expression changed because Swati knew that Trisha was already facing a lot of insecurities, and when she learned about this fact, she got broken. After thinking about that half hour, she came to the conclusion that she had to face this right now, whether it was two days later, one week later, or one year later. so she decided to tell her. She picked up her phone and called Trisha. After two rings, Trisha picked up the call and said "Hello Shefali, how are you?". Shefali replied "Well, I have bad news for you", Trisha said, "What happened? Is it related to Vasant?", Shefali replied "A kind of yes". Trisha, in a scared voice, asked, "Is he alright?", Shefali said "Well, I am directly coming to the point; he has someone else in his life; many of our classmates saw a girl holding the hand of Vasant, walking in the garden", Trisha's heart sinking by hearing those words, she said, "How can this be possible? If he is so true and good to me, then why? I will call him and ask, Maybe there is any confusion," and Trisha cuts the call. Then, without waiting a second, she started calling Vasant. Where Vasant saw the call of Trisha, he got scared and thought no to accepting the call, but suddenly, he decided to pick up the call and took the call and said, "Hello Trisha. Today, his voice is not even comforting her, and she asked "How are you, Vasant?", Vasant replied, "Everything is alright, and what about you? Trisha, in a sober voice, replied "I don't think so". Vasant said, "Why? What happened?", Trisha said Nothing, but I just feel that you don't love me anymore, because I can see that now you have time for everyone to take hand in hand and walk in the park, but there is not even a minute to call and ask if I am fine or not, if I have eaten something or not, whatever no matter how much I am going through, you have neglected everything about me for someone else.". Vasant was shocked by Trisha's words, and now he knows that she knew that he was walking in the park with Shefali. Now he decided to tell her the truth, and he said, Trisha, I want to tell you something". Trisha got scared because she knew what he was going to say. where he said, Trisha, from last week to last week I have decided to go on a trip, where Nishad, Shefali, me, and you are going out for that trip. But when I asked Nishad for the trip, he refused because he was not fine. You also refused because your mother didn't allow you. So I decided to go out with Shefali, and in the evening it suddenly started raining, and we weren't able to come back on the same day from the hills, and it was raining so heavily that we had to stay there in a Hotel. Because the roads have become so slick, I was compelled to make that choice. In between the whole process and travelling, I somehow fell in love with Shefali. I tried not to catch those intentions, but that happens. I am sorry, but I didn't love you any more,", Trisha started crying, and now she is speechless and she can't control her emotion, and she started crying loudly on the call, and it seems so emotional, and Vasant knows that she is very emotional and she will cry, but he has no solution regarding this, and he said "Hey Trisha, don't cry; please stop, and I am saying please stop". Trisha said, "I can't live without you; why don't you understand?" and that whole night they discussed everything with sober tears. Trisha is sounding like a helpless puppy who isn't able to leave his owner. On the other side, Shefali sounding like a selfish cat, Shefali thought that Vasant hadn't called him. Well, it is okay; he might be busy, and she called her other friend to talk. Trisha started counting the minutes because these also seem so long right now.

The next morning, Trisha made a phone call to Vasant and said, "What do you think? Is I am a fool or someone who didn't know that in hiding your ethics, you were talking to that witch Shefali, and do you have any idea what you have done to me? You cheated on me. I thought you were just stupid, but I never thought you were a cheater either. You ditch on me, and you behave like everything was going correctly. You only seem insane, but in actuality, you are a bastard who lies to me everything and every time." After listening to all of this, some words like a knife crushed his ego, and he said "You want to know why I have chosen her over you?", Trisha replied "Yes, Because you are a liar, and you lie every night, and your every promise was fake". Vasant replied to this and said "No, because you didn't leave any option in front of me". Trisha shouted "Are you blaming me for this", Vasant replied, "Leave it; I don't want to discuss anything about that," and then again, a rude conversation happened where they ended with no conclusion. So now Vasant decided that since I left her, there was no need for further communication, and he blocked her number and started doing his daily task. After an hour, there is a call from Shefali, and she says, Vasant, you haven't received my call yesterday; why?", So Vasant tell everything about last night and said "finally I breakup with her", that makes Shefali quite happy and she said "Yeah that was so good, atleast now everything is clear in between us, otherwise I was so tense becuase of her", Vasant said "Don't worry now you are my love and I will take care of each and everything" and than they start discussing about further things and after that within the acedemics and talk the whole day passed in peace for Vasant and Shefali, but Trisha is holding all her eulogy in her heart and doing everything and try to adjust with the situation without tear.

Now Vasant doesn't love her, but still, she has a heart that loves Vasant, and that is where she is stuck; she can't unlove him due to her emotional and faithful approach towards him. Slowly, time started passing, and the closeness among Shefali and Vasant increased, but nobody cared about the fragile heart of Trisha. Her insecurities are increasing with time, and nothing that can heal the pain of separation. it will exist in this universe. We only move forward with that pain, but it always stays somewhere in the subconcious brain, and whenever something hits that, the subconcious brain gets activated and gives you the same feeling of being heartbroken. Every human has been through this pain at least once.

After a week, Trisha called Swati, and In between the talks, she got sober and asked to Swati, "What is special about her that Vasant has left me for her? Yeah, she is more beautiful than me; she has a good body figure and good work ethics; it feels like I don't have anything", Swati replied. "The special thing is not in the human being, but in the sight of the person who is seeing that. you don't have to judge or compare yourrself to her. She has her own good and bad qualities, and you also have the same; try to engage yourself in work; otherwise, you become sober again". Trisha replied, Okay, I will try. Bye,"" and she cut the call.

The sadness was reflecting on the face of Trisha, where everyone around her notices that fact about her, but no one has the courage to ask her. Trisha's mother, Mrs. Sen, also noticed her sadness, and she said, Trisha, I have made a mix of vegetables, pulses, chappati, and rice for you. I also arranged for you to have salad and your favourite mango pickle. Trisha passed a fake and sad smile and said "I am not hungry right now; I will eat after half an hour, mother". Mrs. Sen replied "Okay, Trisha, go upstairs, take a rest, and eat when you feel hungry; I will serve for you".

Now similarly into lonliness, the days started passing. She didn't need to share her time with anyone, so she started working on her habits and lifestyle. where she started learning new things to be more creative and knowledgeable. Even at this work, every barren night is lonely, where the water from the eyes reaches the ears and the murmuring sounds of loved ones are heard.

Now there are no conversations, good laughs, or discussions going on, but still, hopes are living in the heart that one day he will come back and then they will have long talks. Those hopes are somewhere killing her like poison, but every sufferer has a dream that good days will come back. Now she decided to try to call once again, so she dialled the number, but she was still not picking up the call. Instead, she realised that he has blocked her, so she put her phone down. Now she has decided that she will control herself and not try to call him again and again like a despo. Now a chapter of Shefali has started in the life of Vasant.

Shefali is actually a bold woman. She is clever enough to deal with each and every situation. She loves her work ethics and was a beautiful woman who loves to be photographed, so she started modelling on a small scale. She is an influential woman who inspires and motivates others to do their work. But she didn't have great beliefs about love, but she felt too attracted to Vasant, and she liked her life with him.

Shefali has a Close friend named Reeta, who used to date guys to make money and live a luxury life. Shefali was not like that, but Reeta always influences her to follow that path.Everyone in the class of Shefali knows Reeta, who dates guys for their luxury and then leaves them. So mostly her classmates don't like her, but Shefali is a little different, and she notices that nobody wants to become friends with Reeta. So she thought, Reeta felt so alone in the class, and only bad guys used to become friends with her, and then they dated with Reeta, and then after some time Reeta left each of them or they left Reeta. So Shefali found this weird, but weird things attract, and that is how Shefali and Reeta became friends. Her non-judgemental approach towards her friends makes Shefali a brighter personality, and she is too different. Trisha and her beauty have a charismatic magic that attracted Vasant as well.

The similarities between Vasant and Shefali are that they are trying for their own betterment. After dating Shefali, Vasant started going to clubs every weekend night. Where the glamorous look of Shefali is highly admired by the Vasant, his inner urge didn't allow him to let her wear those hot dresses but because he had chosen a girl who is independent of others thought processes so he don't say anthing. She was not just vibing with him and Vasant didn't want to drink alcohol, so he refused to do that always, and that offended Shefali, and she said "Of course it's your choice, but it is not bad if you consume it sometime", Vasant replied "I really didn't want to touch it, but I don't have any problem; you can enjoy", Shefali got drunk, enjoyed it, and danced with Vasant and Reeta. Where Reeta is in search of a rich guy, Shefali is still dancing with Vasant, and after that, Vasant drops Shefali and Reeta at home and goes back. In those lonely moments, when Shefali gets drunk with friends and Vasant sits alone because he doesn't want to drink, he remembers her selfless Ex-girlfriend, who enjoys tea with Vasant and doesn't judge him for being simple, and that moment makes him remember that he promised her that he would always be there for her, but now he can't. But still, he loves the mediaeval version of Shefali that attracts Vasant, and he likes the way she is.

The relationship between Vasant and Shefali is so mature. now Vasant started missing the childish behaviour that she doesn't adore. So one day Vasant asked Shefali "Hey, Shefali, you never feel childish from inside; I love your maturity towards everything, but I want to know what your childish dreams are that you still want to adore". Shefali replied, "Vasant I lost my mother at a very young age, and after that, Dad left me for someone he loved. Because I don't like my stepmother, I decided to live separately from her. So Dad sometimes comes to me, and the only relationship left between us is money. So that's why I started working as a model; it's not only my passion but also need cause they just able to complete my nessisity but now my wishes, so it's a necessity for me. My father sometimes sends me money but sometimes not. and the lifestyle of models needs to be high. but I didn't want to become like a modern model who lives in a metropolis; instead, I live on the outskirts of this city to capture nature and semi-classical vintage modelling pictures to create a difference". Vasant replied, "You are such an inspiring person; I like it! But I think I have asked you the wrong question, I guess. I hope I haven't hurt you". Shefali replied, No, no, it makes me so strong; it makes me mature, so this thing doesn't hurt me anymore because I accept it. Acceptance has the power to heal and to make things natural, no matter how big the problem is". Vasant said, "Okay, it is getting late. Shefali replied, Let me drop you off at your home, and if your parents don't live with you, Can I come to stay with you? Shefali replied "No, I have a smaller brother; I have to take care of her". Vasant said "Well, okay, even if I complete all my work in that time, I will come to meet you after class".

After class, when Shefali has completed her shoot and Vasant has also completed their project on which he is working, in the evening they meet and enjoy, where Vasant says, Shefali, can we go somewhere else for a small date? Shefali agrees with this fact and says, "Yeah, so where can we go?". Shefali said "I know one beautiful place here; let's sit behind me". In the moonlighting, Shefali took him to the lakeside, where they sat, and Shefali and Vasant sat on the bench to enjoy the serene beauty. Shefali placed her head on Vasant's shoulder. They enjoyed that meal together. Then evening turn into night and they went back.

Like this three months passed away with happiness and enjoyment, for Vasant and Shefali. but one day, a message came on the mobile phone of the Vasant. In the message, it is written "Stay Away From My Girlfriend, Otherwise Consequences Are Going To Be Bad ". After reading that, suddenly Vasant got shocked, and he asked "Who are you?", That unknown guy replied "I am Sagar, Shefali's Boyfriend". Vasant replied, "Are you mad? She is my girlfriend", That unknown guy, Sagar, replied "I have to prove that I am his real boyfriend", Vasant replied "Okay, then show me",

Sagar said "I have sent you on your phone", where he sent all the couple pictures that they had clicked together, and some pictures were vulguar and illicit also. When Vasant saw all that stuff, he was shocked and embarrassed that he had loved the wrong girl and he burnt in anger. and In the morning he went to Shefali's house, where Vasant started knocking on the door loudly, and Shefali came to the door hurriedly and said "Oh, Vasant, you are here early in the morning.", Vasant asked, "Where is your brother?". Shefali replied "He had gone to school". Vasant then shouted over Shefali and said "Who is Sagar?", When Shefali heard his name, she became speechless, and her face was down. Vasant shouts again, "Who is Sagar? Tell me!". Then he took her phone and searched for the number of Sagar, where he found his name in the favourites of the list. Vasant said, "Tell me everything; otherwise, I am going to call him," and Vasant started showing him the pictures, and then Shefali realised that Vasant knew everything about them. So she said, "Okay, I will tell you everything. Actually, I tell you a lie that I haven't dated anyone; I am casually dating Sagar for my support system, but when I saw you, it seemed like a true love kind of thing to me but because I didn't believe in true love, so I thought to try it out with you. That's why, from the start, I am trying to attract you, and I just thought if I tell you about Sagar, maybe you don't want to be mine. Vasant said, "Although you didn't tell the truth, if I neglect this fact also, then why is that guy referring to himself as your boyfriend right now? It means you are still casually dating him also?" Now Shefali is speechless and says, "I am sorry. I was dating him for a long time, and he is my ex-boyfriend, but I still like to meet him sometimes. I am sorry, I tried but I just can't. but now I can make everything right for you. I can leave him for you". Vasant replied, " I have asked you about your past, at that time you have to tell everything to me. But you are a liar, so you have chosen to lie to me, and I can't trust a person who lied to me from the start. you know Shefali I realise the relationship but built from lies will fall one day anyhow anytime.". Vasant leaving that place and Shefali tried to stop him, but at that time he was very angry, and his eyes are red, which makes Shefali so afraid of her. Shefali gets so Scared that she knows what will going to happen, but Vasant just goes away, and Shefali follows him until he reaches home. When he entered his flat, Shefali also came and started beating the door. and she was crying and saying, "Open the door!" She said those same words again and again. After some time, Vasant opened the door for her, and she entered and said If I am saying that I am sorry, then why are you creating a Scene?", Vasant got Shocked and said, "The pot calling the kettle black, great, Shefali, great! I have left Trisha for a liar; that's what's making me feel so upset". Shefali replied "I am much better than her; I think she is not even someone with whom you can compare me". Vasant shouted, "Shut up and leave my home; from now on we are strangers. Just keep away from me!" And by that, a sad wind blew in the hearts of both Vasant and Shefali; where they inspire, there is so much to do together, but a lie broke everything between them. Now Shefali realises that cheating on him was the wrong decision she made for Sagar. He sent all the close and illicit pictures of them to Vasant for just a proof, even though Sagar was not worthy, so Shefali tried a lot to stay with Vasant, but because that lie broke Vasant a lot, he was quite shut down, and he refused Shefali for everything, and slowly, with miscommunication, their relationship ended on a Sad note. Vasant has learned a lot about life and about people. The things were not strange, and Vasant noticed that whatever was going on around him, he was not aware of it.

Things between them ended after a week, so Vasant sat with tea in the garden one evening. Where he notices that things happen because he was absorbing everything and he realises that somehow he cheated on Trisha and Shefali cheated on him, that's not very natural; it's much more about Karma. I broke Trisha's heart, and Shefali broke my heart. Well, now I can't trust anyone else than Trisha, and Suddenly in the Garden Nishad came, and he said, Vasant, with whom are you talking? I can't see anyone.". Vasant's eyes were down, and he now looked more sad, and then Nishad understood that there was something wrong with him and that he was sad for some reason. So Nishad asked Vasant, "What happened?" and Vasant replied "Nothing, just nothing". Nishad replied "Brother, you are not to enjoy here; I think Trisha said something bad to you; can you now tell me". Vasant got frustrated and said "I am saying to you again, there is nothing". After trying many times, slowly Nishad convinced Vasant to share his problem, and then Vasant said, "You know our friend Shefali from our Tuition", Nishad said, "Yeah, that hot lady? Of course I know her". Vasant continued, "I started loving her after that trip, and for her, I left Trisha. Because I never felt compatible with Trisha, and with Shefali, everything was exciting and enthusiastic, So I started dating her, and for that reason, I left Trisha, and I have hurt her a lot.", Without listening to the whole thing, Nishad replied, "Oh, you are sad because you left Trisha and you hurt her. Well, there is nothing wrong with choosing Shefali, because you can't live with someone your whole life with whom you never feel good, as you say, because of her clumsy attitude towards her body and your not feeling compatible with him. You are not perfect with him, and you can't spend your whole life with her", Vasant said. "You are right, my friend; I didn't do anything wrong; I just left her from my burden and expectation to be perfect, because I never look perfect with her, and there is nothing wrong with that, and I think that same applies to me; I may not be compatible with Shefali too, which means that God takes away the things that are not good for us. Now I am feeling so free. Thank you, brother, for making me feel okay and listening to me". Nishad replied "Oh, it means you left Trisha for dating Shefali, and he left you for dating someone else" and he burst out into laughter and said "Karma, brother, it's Karma". Vasant made a disgraceful face. Vasant said, "Yeah, you laughed enough; now can you stop joking with me?" and Vasant felt joy in being free, and he said, "Now I don't have to listen to anyone; now I can sleep right now." Now I can do whatever I want, and whenever I want, there is no obligation to take care of someone else, he said, and in happiness, he just jumped, and Everything just restarted again. But the chapter on Shefali has closed.

CHAPTER SEVEN

MARRIAGE PROPOSAL

Now from School life, Vasant entered college life, where everything is so dreamy, and he left Nishad and that place because he got selected for the most prestigious university in India. In that university, when Vasant first entered, after filling out all the details and forms and completing all the formalities, a guard took him to the Hostel, where he found that there were three beds in a room and two huge boys were sitting, one was beige colour and the other one was fair. The imagination of Vasant made him feel that one was similar to a panda and the other was similar to a brown bear, but Vasant keep this thought in his mind only. After that, Vasant put the luggage to one side and said "Hello. The first conversation that happened was Hey, new boy, what is your name?". Vasant replied "I am Vasant, and what about you?", and they both started laughing at him and said Sarcastically "We are aliens, not from this planet", Sarcastically, Vasant Replied "I don't think so; look at yourself", and they got surprised and said "What do you mean by that?". Vasant laughed and said, "Well, nothing," and then a seed of friendship was ripe on this day between those three, and then they replied, "I am Satish, and he is Shiv; welcome, rommie," and that's how their friendship started. Shiv replied "Oh, it's mess time, and I am hungry; let's go". Satish replied "Shiv's hobby is being foody, and he can eat all day". Three of them started laughing over this, and then Shiv replied to this and said, "Satish's hobby is sleeping on weekends; he woke up at lunch time, and I took double breakfast, one for mine and another on the name of Satish," and the three of them started laughing and then went to the mess for food, and after that, in introducing and talking, the whole day ended.

When Vasant left Shefali, rumours passed from friends to friends, and that is how they reached Swati and from her to Trisha. Now Trisha's mind builds the hope that Vasant will come back to her. She spontaneously made a phone call to Vasant, who picked up the call, and Trisha said "Hello, Vasant", Vasant after hearing this melissmatic sound felt relaxed, cause he heard this sound after a bunch of months. His emptiness is covered by the melodic words of her. where he picked up the call and said "hey, have you missed me?", Trisha replied "a lot more than you know", Vasant said "me too, feeling empty, I am not saying that you except me now, but at least you have called me, that is very comforting," and slowly the conversation moves forward. Now Trisha wants that same love back, but Vasant is not sure about that. So one day a conversation was going on and where Trisha asked "Vasant now you left Shefali, so do you want to come back in the same realtionship with me?", Vasant said "I am not sure about it Trisha, I want some time", Trisha said "take your time but remember, I will be yours for always", Vasant said "Trisha don't say that, it makes me feel akward, you know it puts me in a akward situation ", Trisha said "even when you leave me still, I am not able to leave you, why don't you understand". Vasant said, "I am getting your point, dear, but at least give me some time to think about this." Trisha replied "Well, okay, take your time", and somewhere Satish and Shiv were observing this call. cause They started going to Canteen together and, after college, spent time with each other. So many times Satish and Shiv realised that there was a girl who use to called Vasant, and then one day Satish asked, "Who is calling you Vasant at midnight? It seems that something strange is going on with you", Vasant's face was blushing, and he said No, he is my best friend Nishad; he used to call me anytime", And then Satish and Shiv replied Sarcastically together,

"Oh, best friend??, are you pranking infront of us" and they laughed out and refuse to believe in his joke. Where Trisha is the one who is calling Vasant. Satish replied, Well, I guess Nishad sounds like a female," and Vasant said, "Well, why are you both keeping an eye on me? Go away". They both moved out and said, "Yeah, we are already going to mess, and we don't disturb you, right, Shiv," and they vanished.

The next day, Satish and Shiv came and said, Vasant, listen to one thing." Vasant said, "Yeah, speak". Satish said, "Vasant, listen to one thing. It's funny, but yeah, we have heard all what you said yesterday," and Vasant said, "Idiots, you both are crazies." They laughed over this also, and then they said "Now tell us about the whole thing". Now Vasant explains all the things that happened. Satish said, "It means you have dated twice and still the doors of love are not closed from both sides, it is just like neither open nor close. Well played", Now three of them are laughing, and Vasant becomes famous among Singles and gets acclamation. Vasant now feels like a king in the room. but some other boys treat him like a playboy. Now getting a disclaimer of both, Vasant felt awkward about the critics, but everyone has those.

Now he tells all about the situation with Satish and Shiv. After that, Vasant asks, "Do I need to choose her yet, let her go away, or accept her drawbacks". Shiv said "You are talking with her daily, and she cares about you; if you are not in a relationship, it also feels that way,", and Satish gave his suggestion. See, as per your reason, you left her because you don't love her anymore. I think you are just trying to fulfil your emptiness in your heart and nothing else". Vasant is now very confused in that situation and within that time. One day in the evening at six, Trisha make a phone call suddenly to Vasant and said, Vasant, I have something important to discuss with you," and Vasant said, "Yeah, we can. Okay, say it now", Trisha replied. "I've come to know that my family has eyes on a guy for me, but I love you. So now what can I do?", Vasant said. "Will you tell him? and Trisha replied "Yes". Now Vasant thought, What a loving girl is she? and she was going to tell her parents. Vasant said "I want to keep this relationship and want to love you again".

Now again, they unite. They started having love talks again, and now Vasant has decided not to leave her. Trisha's mom again came and said to her, "Trisha We were looking for your father's friend, Uncle Pranav's son, so that you both could get married. We decided to fix your engagement after this year. Trisha said ''mother I want to say something", Mrs Sen replied "yeah tell me, my daughter have grown up and I am so happy for you", Trisha said "Maa I love someone, he also loves me", Mrs Sen get angry over this and said "from how much time ?", Trisha replied "from last four years I am in love with him, he also loves me". Mrs. Sen replied, "Okay, show me his photograph." Trisha opened her phone and showed a picture of him. Mrs. Sen replied, "He is fit and fine, and you are fatty and obese; why does a guy like him like you when he has a lot of choices?. I'm never going to accept him at any cost, and what about his respect? Did you have any idea about our reputation?" , Trisha started crying, and Mrs. Sen also got emotional, but she knew that her Father is a very respected man, and he is the one who lives on their words, and he already gave his words to someone, so Mrs. Sen tried to look strict and hide her emotion in that process, where she said to Trisha, "Your father already has decided something for you."

Now again, they unite. They started having love talks again, and now Vasant has decided not to leave her. Trisha's mom again came and said to her, "Trisha We were looking for your father's friend, Uncle Pranav's son, so that you both could get married. We decided to fix your engagement after this year. Trisha said "Mother, I want to say something", Mrs. Sen replied "Yeah, tell me, my daughter has grown up, and I am so happy for you", Trisha said Maa, I love someone; he also loves me", Mrs. Sen got angry over this and said "From how much time?", Trisha replied "From the four years, I have been in love with him; he also loves me". Mrs. Sen replied, "Okay, show me his photograph." Trisha opened her phone and showed a picture of him. Mrs. Sen replied, "He is fit and fine, and you are fatty; why does a guy like him like you ?, It is so hard to believe,but when he has a lot of choices, why you?, I'm never going to accept him at any cost, and what about his respect? Did you have any idea about our reputation?, what about your father" , Trisha started crying, and Mrs. Sen also got emotional, but she knew that her Father is a very respected man, and he is the one who lives on their words, and he already gives his words to someone, so Mrs. Sen tried to look strict and hide her emotion in that process, where she said to Trisha "Your father already has decided something for you", Trisha felt deep down bad about what happened, and she ran away to her room, where she started crying with heavy tears, because only she knows how much dedication and consistency it takes to bring him back to his life. That day was the biggest sorrow for her because, in her heart, she felt that the hope of living with him had been cut in halves. She knew that her father was very Strict, so her heart was unable to fought against the decisions of her parents.

She is physically present everywhere; she is talking with Vasant. Everything seems alright. But mentally, she is suffering from anxiety because she is not capable of losing her love, and that thought process is making her weak and careless. It seems like she's doing everything with half the efficiency of her brain. When Anubhav came to know about this situation and Mrs. Sen told him about the talk that happened between Trisha and her, he knew that now she was feeling so broken and messed up. She went to her room and knocked on the door. Trisha opened the door and said "Hey, do you need anything?", Anubhav replied "I want to talk to you". Trisha said "About what?", Anubhav replied "Trisha mom, tell me about everything". Trisha yelled at her "Oh, why do I have to tell that to mom". Anubhav said Listen, don't take any wrong steps without my permission. If you're feeling bad about anything, come to me, not to him" . Trisha replied, "I feel comfortable when I talk to him; how can I feel that same way with you? Anubhav said "Everybody needs to gain that power to be strong, and you also, because Father has fixed your marriage with a better guy, who is rich and wealthy, than Vasant, and I don't think that you betray everyone of us in the family for a boy who left you in the middle and then came back". Trisha replied "How do you know that?",

Anubhav replied, "Who doesn't know about that? .Your sad face tells everyone that he left you, or you both have something wrong". Trisha replied "Oh!!". Anubhav said "Okay, I am going for dinner; you can also come and join". Trisha said "I am not hungry, and she turns her face". Anubhav got angry because she turned her face and said "Yeah, keep starving".

Anubhav went back downstairs, and Trisha was still sitting in her room, holding her emotions. A few days passed in sadness.

Now in this first year of graduation, they are both exploring things, and now Vasant's Semester break starts. He goes back home, and the first thing he wants is to meet Trisha. So after reaching there, he called Trisha for the date, and after a lot of months, today Trisha is out with a happy face; she forgot all of her pain and the words of her mother. Vasant takes her to the riverside, and they have enjoyed it a lot. After that, on the same day, Mrs. Sen was also out. She also went to Riverside at the same time. She went there for peace and calmness, and then Mrs. Sen started searching for a bench to sit on. In that, she saw a girl and boy sitting together, and she said to herself, "What a kid nowadays. Parents don't care about their children now; they focus on their own lives. Wait a minute, this pink and white line, this T-shirt, is of Trisha; oh, that girl is Trisha," she says, hurriedly going towards them and putting her hand on the shoulder of that girl. When she looks back, she sees her mother, and they both get shocked, and an uneven and awkward moment arises. Now Mrs. Sen boldly raises her voice and asks, "What is going on, Trisha?", Trisha also gets shocked, and she says, Maa, I am actually! actually!" and she is a little speechless. So Vasant took the lead and started giving explanations, but then Mrs. Sen said, "Take your words back; I am not interested in talking with you," and she took Trisha with her and went away.

Vasant knew the situation was very critical, and he also got away, and they both didn't call each other for many days. After a few days, Vasant thought to connect. With shaking hands, she called her, and after two rings, she picked up the call and said "How are you?" and he said "I am well, and what about the situation?", Trisha said "Well, everything is alright, but Maa is talking a little less; might be she feels weird about that day or may not". Vasant said, "So what is your mother's decision? Is she will going to accept me? Trisha replied Well, that is so typical, I guess, but I try to convince her again and again; maybe she will agree", Vasant said "Yeah, you are so loving and caring". Trisha replied "Yeah, I know" and she started smiling at the compliment and said "Well, let's see when everything gets alright". Mrs. Sen didn't discuss anything about this topic with her, and slowly, a few months passed, and now it seems things have started getting normal. Mrs. Sen didn't talk about that because she wanted to forget it and because she again wanted to normalise things and make things alright. In a few days, Trisha's father, Mr. Sen, talked with her, so she didn't discuss it with her father because she knew that he was very strict in this situation and that he believed in the caste system, so he would never allow Trisha to do that. She thought that she would handle her on her own. After a few days, when everything was alright, Trisha again started having conversations with Vasant. Within the conversation, Vasant said, "Trisha, I am having a Diwali Break. Can I come to meet you", Trisha got scared, and she said "I will try, and now this time, please try to find a distant place, okay", Vasant said "Okay.". Again, she dressed well, but her heart was scared, and this time she didn't want to take any risks. So she thought to take the help of Anubhav, and she said, "Brother, Listen, I am going to meet Vasant, and after all of these months, everything has normalised. If she finds me again with him, she will get mad this time. Will you take care of the situation and help me out?". Anubhav replied, "Did you still love that guy? Well, the best thing you have done is that you told me. Okay, so let's talk about him" and then Anubhav continued and asked, "Tell me his surname and Caste". Trisha replied "He never told me about that, and I even never asked him about that". Anubhav said, "Are you mad? You are loving a guy from the last two or three years, and you don't know his surname?". Trisha replied, "he never told me about that" . Anubhav got scared and said "Okay, you go and meet him, and also ask his surname, and remember we are brahmins, and if he is of a lower caste than us, our father is never going to accept him". Trisha got shocked and said Ahh, that's awful; this is not fair". Anubhav replied, "There is nothing anyone can do for this! Even if Father allows, he also has to face society, and I am sure that he is not going to agree", Trisha's face dulls, and she puts all of her courage into it and says, "Now it feels hard to meet him, because the moment I ask the question, everything tends towards ending, I guess", and then Trisha leaves her home and goes to the place from where he can pick her up. Trisha went out with her to a monastery, and in the calmness, they both sat. where Vasant notices that she seems a little scared and anxious. Vasant said, "Why are you restless, Trisha? What happened?", Trisha replied, "Well, it is hard to ask something right now." Vasant said, "If you find asking something hard, it might be about Shefali. Well, don't worry, just ask, and if you don't feel comfortable, take you time". Trisha replied "No, I am also curious, so I have to ask", Vasant replied "Oh, if it is something that much more necessary than ask it now", So Trisha said Okay, so tell your surname and category in which you fall.", Vasant said "Well, I am prajpati by surname, and I fall in OBC category, which is another backward caste; anything else?", Trisha's heart got broken, and she got shocked and said No, there's nothing else left to discuss". She stood on her place and said, Let's go; I didn't feel alright", Vasant said to Trisha, Listen, are your parents narrow enough that they will not let us marry due to the caste system? ", Trisha told him, "My brother stated to me that if he is not a brahmin, just leave him from the thought of getting married, so you are not a brahmin, and this will break all my dreams of getting married with you. It feels like love is not enough, and you are not employed; there is nothing that can make this impossible situation possible. She started crying and then said, "Hey, stop crying! Please stop crying!" Trisha glued her tears to her eyes, but the pain in her heart was unbearable. She stopped for a few minutes and then again started crying. Vasant gave sympathy to her, and then Vasant said "I have an idea", Trisha said "What?", Vasant said "You need to wait one or two years for that", Trisha said "Okay, tell me", Vasant said,

"After one or two years, I will get employed, and then my mother will come to take your hand, but at least you have to wait for two years. How can you say yes to an unemployed guy". Trisha stopped crying and said, "Okay, I will wait for you!" and then happily once again she went home, but still she was nervous, but her happiness was overpowering because Vasant had promised her.

Now Trisha has started their long-distance relationship, they keep talking, laughing, and enjoying themselves together. The long distance didn't even feel long. Like that, years passed.

Next year, Vasant enters the job market and interviews. Where Vasant started trying to find employment, and Vasant was preparing well and trying very hard to make his place in the job. After giving a lot of exams and interviews, Vasant still didn't get selected, and now the situation was going against Vasant and Trisha. Where Trisha's parents start building pressure on her for marriage, where she is not responding to anyone of them, and on the other hand, Vasant is trying to get a decent job. Like that, he entered into third year, but Trisha pressured him, and a conversation about this happened.

After a few days, Trisha made a call to her. and Vasant picked up and said "Hey, how are you?", Trisha said, "Vasant listen, it's very crucial, my parents started looking for my groom, and every time,I use to refuse, they question me and it will get so weird and you know It's getting complicated day by day, please do something regarding to this . So Vasant said Well, within this month I am trying, I can see that you are scared. Okay, let me convince my mother", Trisha said "Well, I will manage for a few months; don't worry. By listening to those words, Vasant got relaxed, and slowly, with time, he entered in the last year of graduation, and now Vasant was more confident for the interviews and job applications. His self-confidence was reflected in his actions when he gave those interviews. When Trisha talks to Vasant, she feels that confidence and she loves that confidence. Finally, Vasant cracks the interview after a lot of hard work and excellence in academics. They First called Mrs. Indra ji and said "Maa, I got the job; where is papa?",

Mrs. Indra ji said, "Well done, my child! Today, I am very proud of you! I am giving him the phone; talk to him." He took the phone and said, "Congratulations, my son! I have heard everything from your mother; my blessings are with you. Keep achieving", and then Vasant said "Thank you!, thank you!, papa, take care of Maa and yours, okay, and I will call you in the evening. bye", and cuts the call. After that, he called Trisha, where Trisha was also eagerly waiting for Vasant, and she said "Hello, Vasant, how are you, your phone was going busy?", Vasant said " leave that, and listen I have something special to tell you", Trisha got excited, and somewhere she knew what he was going to say, but still she was very curious and excited for those words. She said "Okay, tell me; I am very excited to listen to you". Vasant said, Trisha, I got the job; at least now I am capable of handling my own bills and yours. Now I can talk to your mother about our marriage". Trisha got very excited, and she ran from her room to her mother's room to tell her mother that Vasant got employed. Mrs. Sen replied, "Oh, he got the job, that's good for him, but it is not really a matter for me" and by hearing those faded words,she went back to her room. Trisha comes to know that she still does not agree, I guess, and she calls Vasant and starts discussing her faded reaction to this. So Vasant said, "Maybe she was in a good mood; that's why she didn't react. Well, I will tell my mom and convince her to convince your mother" Vasant said. Trisha happily said," Okay, Vasant," and he cuts the call. Vasant came back from college, took a bus, and went back to home. When Vasant reaches home, He first touches the feets of his parents, and they give him blessings. and Then Mrs Indra said "you surpurise us,tell me atleast once, before coming, so I can cook something delicious for you", Vasant replied "Maa you cook everything delicious, and If still it is not delicious it means that there is problem in the raw materials or vegetables" and Mrs Indra get impress by those words and said "hehe !!, okay go to your room and do rest, I will send the food to your room" and then when mother come with food into the room, Vasant said "sit mother, sit here, I will talk to you and also eat the food", So Mrs. Indra sat on the chair and she was looking tired or in discomfort, and then Vasant started pampering her Mom, and said " do you want a head massage?" Mother replied "No, my son, I am fine", Vasant replied, "You are not going to say yes; I have to do with my own will", and he started giving him the head massage with champi oil. Camly Vasant said " Maa I want to tell you, something", Mrs. Indra ji said "Yes, tell me", Vasant replied"I like a girl" and after listening that Mrs Indra ji stand and said "whom? , did i know her?", and then Vasant said "Yes maa a kindoff, I want to tell you that I love Trisha", Mrs Indra get complex over this cause she was fatty and looks very uncompatiable with Vasant but then she thought that Vasant have choosed her in his mature state so she said "Trisha, have you think about it wisely?", Vasant said "yes mother, I know her personality and looks were not what you expected for your daughter in law, but she was so kind and loyal, that makes me took this decision", Mrs. Indra said "If you love her and you think over it so wisely also ,I don't have any doubt on you, Go and get her" ." I agree, because I know her, and I will going to love her, although she looks average in compare to you but yeah!!, let's meet". then Mrs. Indra ji tell this news to his father. she said "your son loves that girl Trisha, he confessed to me and tell me everything,Although that girl Trisha is too average infront of our son but still, she is Vasant's choice, so I am agree with him", after listening those words father said "it's alright, you visit to her house and talk about marriage and don't forget to take the box of sweet" and, she said "okay".Vasant replied "Maa, but I need your help". Mrs. Indra Ji said and then the next day Mrs. Indra prepared her with a beautiful bindi to cheer the moment. she went to Trisha's home. she also wear her gold bangles and jewellery. and then put the bindi in the centre of the forehead and put her vermillion. Everyone knows the reason, and Vasant and her Mother reach Trisha's house.

When Mrs. Sen saw Vasant and his mother, she get burned, but she behave calmly and, Mrs. Sen, as mother of Trisha, very respectfully addresses Mrs. Indra Ji. Vasant went and touched the feet of Mrs. Sen, and she said,"Vasant, God bless you, sit! Anubhav also touched Mrs. Indra's feet; after that, Trisha was not aware that he was coming, she already tells this to anubhav. In her room, she was thinking about why she is unable to tell that to her mother, and she thought she had made a promise to Vasant. In her mind, she is saying "It is easy to promise, but it is hard to keep that promise", She was just collecting everything, and then Anubhav comes and said "Trisha, see that Vasant came with her mother," and Trisha gets scared, and she sits on the stairs and starts listening to everything. Mrs. Indra Ji said "Call Trisha; where is she?". Mrs. Sen replied, "Yeah! Trisha, come down", She said it loudly, and Trisha came down the stairs and Trisha was very scared for all that. Now Vasant's mother said "Mrs. Sen, I think you know Trisha loves Vasant", The expression of her face changed a little, and she said Yeah, Trisha, tell me about that", and she wanted to say something more by cutting her in between. Mrs. Indra said, "So I am here to talk about their marriage; even my son is employed now, on a good and reputable place, and we have a great family; here in our family, everyone is kind and good. I think Trisha stay happy with us", Mrs Sen replied "there is no doubt that Vasant is great person, but Mrs Indra we are bramhins and we don't want to send our daughter to non- Brahmin family, that is why we have already fixed his marriage with someone else, but we didn't tell her yet because we thought, when she get ready for marriage after her studies we tell her and for more information we wants to tell you that our son in law is in army on a officer rank, so I am really very sorry, we can't accept your marriage proposal, I know they love eachother, but everything is not about love and we have maintain the reputation in our society". After hearing the whole things and taunt Trisha and Vasant gets dishearten and they both loose the hope of being together and Vasant saw how Mrs Sen taunt her mother but still he keep silence. After that, Mrs. Indra broke the silence and said, "Although my son loves your daughter, this is the only reason that I came here, but somewhere I know that my son deserves someone much better than her. So Vasant, now you want to say something else, or we should leave?". Vasant said "Mrs. Sen, take your time; don't rush to a decision in this hurry", Mrs. Sen replied "Yeah, I heard your mother say that you deserve someone better, so now I don't have any doubt in rejecting you". Mrs. Indra said, "Vasant, let's go; we can't fix your marriage here, or you want her to feel more criticised," and Trisha got numb, and she lost all those hopes with those hopes she was living. Now Vasant was also crying internally and said, Maa, let's go," and they left their house and went back. Trisha said, Maa, why do you do that with me?", Mrs. Sen replied, "Why have you dated a lower caste guy? ,You have to think about our reputation, and we can't give our daughter to them; What about your father's respect?, this is a fact, and you have to keep this in your mind and if you still want to marry him, so remember ". Now hopes end with the flowing of time like water, where time and relationships have no ends.

Now whole day ended, and Trisha felt like "The hanky of the world that can't wrap up her tears," and from the whole thing, even after trying everything, Tears are the only thing they both get. Now a sad prose has started between them after everything just ended. Trisha's heart can't believe that this is the bitter truth. She somewhere started thinking that she was never going to get that love again because everything ended that way. They both give up and sat down in their situations.

Vasant gets back to his job, and he now really wants to forget her because he knows that he has no future with her. He was assigned the work, and he got busy with his college and job, where he reached about the end because he got a job at the beginning of the last year, so still now he has a lot of time to give more interviews and exams with college, and he again started focusing on himself, but still felt the loneliness created by Trisha's absence. Vasant started realising that he had tried a lot, but only Trisha had loved him the way he did. He left everything because he believes that Trisha is her "True love," and nobody is going to love him in that way. He lost her, but how? Once, he lost her because of his mistake, and Now he has lost her forever. Now those forever promises sounds fake, and the Value of a promise has been calculated by the thoughtfulness of someone else. But there is nothing more sad for a person who has everything but is still not able to protect his love.

95

CHAPTER EIGHT

DIVISION OF LIFE

When everything ended, Vasant started reading the books in his free time and trying to evolve more and more. So after his nine to five Schedule, Vasant sits down on his study table and takes a book and starts reading, where becaustnthat suddenly falls on the floor, So Vasant bend down on which it is written "If you don't like your Story, Change it". After reading that note, a thought jumps into Vasant's mind: maybe something else is waiting for him, and he doesn't deserve this sad ending. Slowly, he tries to do different things to enrich his life. They both are trying to manage things.

After a few days, Trisheunable to manage her emotions, makes a phone call to Vasant, and Vasant feels comforted when he sees the call from Trisha, so tried not to pickup his call, but he unable to control him and he picks up the call and he said "What else is left to say", Trisha replied "Nothing; I just called you because I love you yet", Vasant replied "Oh, that is why you are marrying someone else". Trisha replied "I didn't choose him; my father chose him; what else I can do?". Vasant replied "When everyone is fighting, you are silently sitting on one side; you didn't say a word". Trisha replied, "That time I didn't feel right to say anything because our mother was almost fighting; if I say something, the chances of her saying yes may get lower", Vasant replied, "Oh, there is no chance left now; what would you like to say about that?", Trisha replied, "What can I do for that? I still love you. I know that I am not marrying you, but I still love you. And listen", Vasant replied

"What?", Trisha replied, "Because Vasant, we love each other, so please be mine until I get married. After that situation, separate us; at least be mine until that stage". Vasant replied "No, Trisha, I can't stop for you, because we don't have any future, so it is a waste of time", Trisha screamed in anger and said "Don't you dare to go to someone else, if you ever loved me, so now you can still love me without even marriage", Vasant replied "Why should I love you till your maariage, it seems like a prank to my ears, I also need to move on in my life". Trisha said "Because I love you and I will not let anyone become yours until destiny separates us, even if my parents let me marry him, then I am also going to love you only". Vasant said, "Why do you always talk like an immature woman? Be responsible. After your marriage, you will going to leave me? and So why?", Trisha replied "Because I don't want". Vasant said, "What a girl you are!, If you have to call me for this stupid stuff, don't call me", Trisha said "Oh, your ego comes in between", and after sometime Vasant cuts the call.

Mrs. Sen thought their daughter Trisha has grown up, so now She calls her father. and a conversation goes on. He picked up the call and said "Hello, how are you?". Mrs. Sen responded and said "I am good, but there is something that happens", Mr. Sen said "Tell me what happened,", so Mrs. Sen explained the whole thing that happened. So Mr. Sen said over this, "you done a good job by telling me all of this, from this conversation I come to know that our daughter started rebeling against us, so I decided, that I will come to do engagement of Trisha, giving her more freedom is not right. if it is not right for her," and after this, the conversation ends.

After a few more weeks, a turning point comes in the lives of Vasant and Trisha. Now While serving his duty on a mission, Trisha's father, Mr. Sen, died. The death of Mr. Sen has shaken the whole family; Although Trisha's brother is there to manage the family financially, . Now only the main bills are being managed. Now that Anubhav's marriage has been fixed, but there was no one left to demand. Situation was coming to Trisha, but Now there Slowly, Mrs. Sen started getting sick, and she started suffering from the problem of diabetes. Trisha takes care of her mother's food and medicine. Even though she learns how to inject insulin, she realises there is a lot she needs to do now. a kind of meeting with adulting and realistic problems She realised what life actually is, and now she has started becoming more responsible. Her mother felt alone, so instead of choosing any other person, she chose her mother. Now slowly, they get separated. The unwanted emptiness hurts, but the adulting hurts her more, and she is trying to comfort her mother.

Now she realises the worth of education and herself because the whole day feels so long. But she tried to keep herself busy, but when her heart didn't listen to her, she called Vasant,like time had passed. With the passage of time, Trisha and Vasant get separated. Now they get busy with their own lives.

BEGIN AGAIN

Now in this last year of graduation, everyone was chasing good companies to apply to to get employment, here Vasant trying to upgrade his Job. But he has pain in his heart because now the reason he was searching for employment just vanished. Everything made a great impact on him. Due to his great depth of knowledge in his subjects, everyone knows Vasant, So college teachers have decided to form a community where, Vasant was the head or leader of the community after the teachers. Vasant and teachers work very hard for this community, which basically provides webinars on those subjects. Now juniors were appointed to work in the teams, and Vasant put a notice on the notice board of the college that "if anyone wants to be part of the community, they can assign their name to him". There was a bulk of students giving their names, and only one last-year student enrolled in that. Vasant found that the girl who enrolled was a girl from his class, and she was quite unique among all the girls in the class; she was a little weird, talks less, and just has one friend. He asked, "Did you also come here to apply?", She said, "Yeah! Actually, I didn't get selected anywhere yet, so I thought to join this community to learn". Vasant said, "Oh, you also want to learn, but because you are in your last year, I am putting you in charge of the management of this team also. You learn the management also. Well, I never asked your name in the class". She replied "I am Chitra". Vasant said "Nice name, okay, well, what is your specialisation?" She replied "Well, I don't think so" stu, Vasant said "okay, you can join by tomorrow and help me with further arrangements". Chitra replied "Okay.". Vasant always finds her weird due to her friend circle, but when she talks today, it doesn't feel the same.

She started creating beautiful templates for their webinar and managing everything in the backend. Together, they help the whole community grow. Where Chitra finds him, he does his job so well that he didn't even lunch in the afternoon, so in the break, she said, "Vasant, why didn't you lunch in the afternoon?, You always go to eat in the canteen", Vasant said "I am working on designing the template, so I was busy and am not able to prepare lunch". Chitra said "Well, it's okay; I can share my lunch with you; would you like to?". Vasant likes this kindness with food, and he also starts liking the girl who shares her food. Somewhere, working for the freshers with Chitra help him to fill the emptiness in her heart. Next day when Chitra didn't come to college, and Vasant was preparing notes for a demonstration. After the work at lunch, he saw Chitra was missing today, and his eyes started searching for her everywhere. Slowly not finding her anywhere send him instict, and makes him feel the pain of being alone. He finds that Chitra is a very pretty, kind, and sensible girl who makes him feel better. So when he found her good enough, Vasant started thinking, What if she becomes my girlfriend? In his mind, within building thoughts, he also thought that if she said yes to him, so they could marry with eachother and the thread of hope built after the knot created by Trisha's mother, and this time he didn't take any chance to lose her. So Vasant made a phone call to Chitra, and she found the call from Vasant. She picked up the call and said "Hello Vasant, how are you?", Vasant replied, "I am good, and what about you? Why are you absent today in the workshop?" Chitra replied "Well, I am going home; I think I will prepare at home". Vasant thought if she went away, he would not be able to put the proposal in front of her, and the Case wouldn't move forward. So I became a little anxious, and Vasant said loudly, "Chitra, I am preparing for some interviews; why don't you prepare with me? And if you go back home, then you aren't able to prepare well, because at home things are at ease, and you might be become lazy, so it doesn't work", Chitra replied. Vasant, but I am not lazy like you, and I will try not to be lazy, and actually, I have already booked the tickets, so it's a waste of money. Don't worry, I will come back after a few days ". Vasant felt offended because now he feels that, he was loosing hope, so he said, "Do whatever you want; okay, bye." Chitra found that behaviour to be super weird, but she didn't understand what the matter was with him. She ignored all the facts. She went to the station and took her bus, and within that journey, a message from Vasant appears on the notification of Chitra, and that message is "I want to talk something important about you, may I?" , Chitra pings "Hey, I am travelling and the networks are not well; shall we connect after I reach home?". Vasant replied "Sure, but ping me when you reach home". Chitra replied "Why should I need to tell you". Vasant replied "Well, I just want to ensure that you reach home safely". Chitra found this to be a caring act for her, and she said "Thanks". After that long journey, Chitra reached her home again, and she suddenly remembered that she needed to ping Vasant. She went into her room and ping a message to Vasant, "I reached home safely", and she got off her phone. Vasant wasn't able to see her online. So he waited for some time, but when he saw that she was not coming online,So he put the phone down and started doing his work again. Vasant found out that he had just met her for the last few weeks just as a friend, but still, it seems like his heart doesn't sound okay because now she was not around. That is something Vasant found to be very different about her. He started thinking, "How do I feel alright? but how?". Then an idea reaches Vasant's head, and he calls Trisha and talks to her to discuss what is going on. Trisha also felt very happy when he called her, but Trisha found it be very strange that after a month Vasant was calling suddenly, and she asked "How do you remember me after this time?". Hiding all his stuff, Vasant said "Nothing, I just called you randomly", Trisha felt so mean and said, "You can also say to me that, Trisha, I miss you, so I have called you, but no! You don't care now". Vasant said, "I don't miss you, and everything is over between us; we almost compromised in this situation; what else do you want? Now you are the brilliant Daughter of your parents, for a mother who compell you everytime" and Vasant started taunting her. They both taunted each other and were still fighting over that topic, and then Vasant said "There is no conclusion to that, so I am cutting the call", Trisha replied, "Can we talk like friends?" and Vasant replied, "No, we can't be friends. Okay, I respect you, but I loved you once, and that hurt me a lot, so I don't want to be your friend. You are my Ex girlfriend forever". After a few conversations, Vasant put the phone down. Now he realises That before Calling Trisha, he was happy and in a good mood, and now calling Trisha was not comforting, cause now it didn't feels the same. He realises now that calling Trisha was just like turning the old pages. So he stopped thinking about Trisha and the moment he stop thinking about Trisha, he realise that Chitra is the only name that he wanted to remember, and he started Dreaming with Chitra. Where he wants to make sure that she needs to be a little more courageous. but still, nothing has been started. So the next morning, Vasant ping Chitra and said "Hi" and Trisha started getting to know that there must be something in his mind that he wanted to share, so she replied in a second reply "Hello, how are you?", Where Vasant became extremely happy when he got the reply and said "I am well, and what about you?", Chitra replied "Well, I have done my breakfast, and now I have started my daily routine". Vasant said, "That is so great, Chitra. Can I ask you something?", Chitra said, "Yeah, of course." Vasant asked "Do you have someone special in your life?", Chitra said "Yes", Vasant disgruntledly asked, "Whom?", Chitra replied Well, My mom and dad are very special for me ". This brought a smile to the face of Vasant, and he said "Oh, well, I have a question for you?", Vasant replied "Yeah, they are very special for you; I understand, but I am asking, do you have a soulmate or a boyfriend?", Chitra replied "No, I don't have". So Vasant asked again in excitement, "Really, Than, what qualities are you looking for?" Chitra replied "Um, I didn't know; maybe he needs to be taller,

I guess", Vasant said, Oh, if he is not too tall, than what?" Chitra replied "Well, he needs to be taller than mine atleast, or I look for other things, may be his dress up.", Vasant said, "That is all fine, but what if I want to be your soulmate?, Vasant said "So it is a yes or a no", Chitra is very confused because this was the first time someone has asked this directly to her. So she said "Well, I can try, and without giving you my time, I can say yes or no", Vasant said "So how much time do you want, and after what time will you be officially mine?". Chitra put a smiling emoji and said, Well, for official purposes, you have to ask my father, and I don't know how much time it will take. Vasant thought, It might be she wants to refuse, but she didn't want to say it directly, so I think just leave the situation". Vasant said "Okay, take your time". and then, after a few more talks, they stop the conversation. The last full stop on the message lasted for two to three months, and still they don't talk again. Vasant lost hope, and Chitra is too shy to talk and ping on her own. And Now it's time when exams are about to start and they need to go back to college, so Chitra goes back to college, and because an awkwardness has been created between them, Chitra decides to break that awkwardness, and he pings Vasant and asks, "How are you?", He pings back "I am well, and what about your preparation". Chitra replied, "Well, I have tried enough, but I am still not able to solve these problems and use these tools. Will you help me?", Vasant replied, "Of course, and he said, Fix an online meeting; I will teach you."

After that, Vasant teaches her the whole thing about those tools and how to use them. But she still finds it very difficult, and now she thinks things won't remain awkward. After that, she learned them with her friends, and the next day after the exam, Chitra received a call from Vasant, and he was asking "How was your exam?", Chitra said, "It goes fine, and yours?", Vasant replied "Yeah, I have command over these subjects and tools, so my exam also goes well". Chitra said "Yeah, you are very knowledgeable; I know".

After a good conversation, they cut the calls. Now they want to talk, but they don't. After that gap, Vasant is now very confused about whether she wants to date or not. Chitra was also confused, and she thought, "What an egoistic man! He said he liked me, but now he didn't call me back," and this is how a few more days passed away without any conclusion. Where they met in the winters, That winters turn into hustling Summer, and Summer didn't make anything come into conclusion, but within the end of the Summer, there comes the season of love, that is "MANSOON".

This season brings rain, and Chitra, sitting in her room, waving with the drops of rain, highly complex and happy vibes started revolving in her mind. That compex feeling was hitting her, and now she felt in her mind, "If she had him,in this rain, he would make her feel special, but he was not here, so at least I could call her". But then Chitra thought, This makes him feel that she is still running for him, so she doesn't call. and she thought to go to the library and study some material. After coming from the library, a storm has reached where heavy rain and thunder were coming, but Chitra has studied for a few hours, and now she wants to go back because it is seven in the evening and after some time it will going to become dark. So Chitra thought to take some vehicles, but there were none. Now she started going back home by foot, but she get little scared. And in this situation, she thought to call her mother to inform her, but when she opened the tab, she found the number of Vasant, and she decided to call him immediately. She was about to dial her mother's number, but by mistake, a missed call was just left on the mother's phone by Chitra. So her Mother calls her back, and the phone was busy. So she got confused about who she was talking with. Now Chitra has called Vasant, and Vasant asks, "What happened, Chitra?" So she told him, "Actually, I came to the library, but now it is raining heavily, so I am not getting any vehicles to reach My room." Vasant said "Oh, I am sorry, but I am also out of town, so I can't help you". Chitra said "No, no, actually I didn't want any favour from you, but I felt a little scared, so I called you", Vasant said, "Okay," and then a conversation started that went so long until she didn't reach her home, and after that, Chitra said "thankyou Vasant" and cut the call. When Trisha cuts her call, her mother was also calling her, and when Chitra picks up the call, Mother asks, Chitra, why don't you pick up the call? Your phone was going busy. Chitra made a shy face and said, "No, ma'am, I didn't get your call. It may be because there is heavy rain, so there may be some network issue.". Mother reacted mischeviously and said "Maybe you are calling someone else", Chitra replied, No, mother," and then she told about the heavy storm, and after a good conversation, they cut the call.

Then Chitra went back to her, still watching the same rain alone, and then sat and started introspection, and she found something odd: that there are so many contacts where she can call, but his mind strikes only at Vasant, and then looking at the rain and this little lonliness, she thought, I think he may be the missing piece of my heart. Then she said to herself, "Should I call him? or not", umm well, I think I want to call, and well, I think I want to call, and she again made her choice in the rainy vibe to call Vasant, and Vasant picked up the call, and they started talking, and then Vasant said, "So how's everything and can I ask the reason of remembering my exsistence?" Chitra replied, "That is so great, but I just thought to call you, so I have called you." Vasant replied, "Oh, that is a good decision you have taken." Chitra replied "That is so great, but I just thought to call you,even so I talk very rarely". Vasant replied "You are very different from others, which I found very attractive about you, and when you share your tiffin, I find you very kind and humble, and then I come to know that you are not dating, so I thought to confess this to you", Chitra said, "That's good. Well, I also want confess something". Vasant replied "What?", She said "I love rain; I have so many fantasies; um, well, do you have any?". Vasant replied, "Well, I do have rain fantasies, but my thoughts are encrypted and my girlfriend only use to understand those things", Chitra disgruntedly said" What do you mean?", Vasant replied why should I tell you? I will tell them to my girlfriend", Chitra got jealous by listening to those words, and by making a shy voice, she said "Oh, really, you refused to tell me, but you like me",Vasant said "Yeah but still..........". Chitra said "But what If I feel something". Vasant got shocked into enthusiasm and said, "Really?" , and Chitra realised the feelings that she had for him that she had been unable to unlock for a long time, and she said, "Okay, you can ask me anything today; you have freedom; I will not refuse for anything, and then Vasant asked, Will you be my soulmate? In that moment, the heart rate of Vasant was so high, and he knew what she was going to say, but he didn't want to hear it from her, and then Chitra said, "Yess. Vasant got shocked and jumped into happiness. Finally, he unlocked the box of feelings, and for the first time, Chitra said "I love you", With those words, Vasant lived. Now Vasant has planned an amazing date for her, and when they met, they flowed with each other in the sky of dreams; it was just looking like a dream, and that was the happiest day, when they met first and when they were in love.

CHAPTER TEN

THAT FEBRUARY

Now slowly, ,Mansoon turn into Autumn when every leave fades and when Autumn dissappear winter comes like a cozy blanket, where they started coming close, and day by day, spring started coming, where all the Semal trees started to blossom with the beautiful red flowers near the roads. School children started collecting them to play games with their stamens. On the other side, women also collect them for cooking and serve them as a tasty dish. The red flowers that were left on the trees gave off a serene look against the blue sky. In spring, cotton also yields and starts falling on the green grass that looks similar to snow. Vasant, while going to college, saw that scene of nature, and he decided to bring Chitra here with him. He knows this is what she loves. So the next day after college, Vasant takes Chitra to that garden, where trees are full of raw mango and the whole green grass on one side is covered by cotton flowers. Chitra gets full of joy by seeing the view because it just looks like a miniature painting. They sit on the park bench, where they are dreaming and pampering each other. Chitra puts her head on his shoulder. They are talking little things about each other and giggle and laugh by joking on each other. Chitra brought the lunch box with her because she was coming from college. They shared food and enjoyed it, just like at a picnic. This day was actually a special one. Not for everyone, but yeah, surely for someone who finds someone in their life so special. This day is the Seventh of February, and Vasant has already decided to bring something special to her, and he knows that Chitra loves open places like gardens, so on this day, it is usually more romantic for a new couple. Maybe for some couples, with time, feelings and love fade, but still, some lovers maintain the authenticity of this day. For Vasant and Chitra, this day was so special, because they are going to celebrate it together for the first time. For them in that garden, it feels like Time had frozen and is meaningless because, at that moment, they are not even realising how much time has passed.

So today is "Rose Day," and as it is the first day of Valentine's Week, it gets more attention than other days. Chitra was also aware of why Vasant had called him to the garden, so in the morning she started decorating herself with makeup and accessories to look more beautiful, just like a rose.

Every year on this day, Teenage Chitra always watches couples around, and in her friend circle, everyone gets flowers. She just thinks about that one day when she gets the flowers. With the passing of time in those many years, that day came. That is why, in her bag, she kept a few roses for him. So her expectations for this day was too high. Now back to that moment after all of this: Chitra said, "Vasant, close your eyes" and pick out the flowers. Vasant got amused and so happy for these roses, and suddenly he dropped his keys down and said Chittra, can you pick up the keys for me?", Chitra replied, "Yeah," and she bent down to pick up the keys, and there she found a big bunch of roses on a beautiful floral pink handkerchief, and Chitra got surprised with them and took all of them in her hand and said, "How beautiful are these roses? They are shiny and have big, long petals. Vasant put phrases for creating a jolly moment together and said "Rose in the hand, rose". Chitra felt so shy with his words and then laughed and said "Good flirting skills, Vasant", and Vasant started giggling. They held hands with each other, and they went back. Chitra framed two and three petals of the roses in her personal diary and wrote something about that day, where she wrote all her personal feelings, but the special feeling and glimpses of her note are: Vasant, you make this day so special for me. I love you for making this moment feels so Beautiful". This is how 'Rose Day passed with the aroma of happiness.

PROPOSE ME

Proposals are beautiful; many people get them, some accept them, and others just run away with their lives. That day must be a beautiful day for lovers. Behind every beautiful love story, there is someone who has the courage to start. What is a perfect proposal? It is not something complex to find out because, in every eye and in their personal perceptions, everyone defines a proposal differently. So perfect proposals must be hidden in the sight and virtue of a person, but I think the perfect proposal is something that is in the mind of Vasant for his wife; he dreamed that when he married her, he would propose to Chitra in this and those ways. He has a lot of things on his mind. Vasant is realistic at work but dreamy in love. This time he wanted to surprise her in a different way, but he didn't have any idea what he could done for her. On the other side, Chitra was also confused about what to wear, and suddenly Chitra has reminded of the suit and long skirt set that her mother had brought to her latest, and she was very curious because she knew that Vasant had going to gave him a surprise, but what can it be? So she started getting ready, withholding that curiosity in his mind. where Vasant was busy in finding the best thing for her, so when nothing strikes his mind, he goes out to the Market, where, while rotating his eyes and searching for gifts, Vasant goes to a gift shop. There, after seeing everything, the shopkeeper shows him some beautiful rings, and Vasant buys one for her. But still, Vasant is not satisfied; he goes out to shop, still thinking about it, and after the junction of three roads, when he moves forward, he saw a bakery shop. That bakery was so aesthetically decorated with a Valentine's day theme; the porch is covered with red balloons, and they are selling them also. So Vasant went into the bakery, where the lady in the bakery greeted him. He liked it a lot that someone was talking to him so gracefully, and she said "Sir, what do you like to order?", So Vasant said "Well, I want something for my girlfriend for propose day", so that lady said to him, Well, sir, you can impress her with a themed cake on propose day; sir, if you put an order, we will also have home delivery available", Vasant said,Ooh, that is a great idea; I think she gets impressed with that." Thaat lady said, Sir, do you give any idea of what you want to represent on the cake, any theme", and after thinking for a few minutes, an idea struck in the head of Vasant, and in that, you put this ring. That lady liked the idea of Vasant, and she judged his character as a caring and loving person. Then she asks "Sir, what do you want to write on the cake, anything like love, soulmate, or anything?", After thinking for a few minutes, a poetic line suddenly strikes the mind of Vasant, and he replies to her "Okay ,Will you be my soulmate?', I think this is perfect". She asks him again "Sir, do you want frosting on this cake and cake toys of different looks?", Vasant replies, No, I don't think so; I think the cake will look overfilled, so don't put frosting on the cake". She replied, "Okay, sir". Then Vasant asked her "well, can you deliver this so that I can surprise her, or do I have to come?", She replied," Sir, we can deliver it to your address, but It will take some extra charges; are you willing to pay?". So Vasant very confidently replied "Of course, Sure, I will ping you the address later", That bakery Woman replied, Okay, Sir, thank you so much for your order; come again next time". and now Vasant was so happy that he has prepared that surprise for her. He goes back home and Cause Mrs. Indra Ji was not at home, he decided to go with a non-expensive celebration and decided to organise the backyard and put up balloons, and decorate the garage room, which is very dirty right now, so Vasant goes to his younger brother and ask him to clean that place with him, both brothers started working and cleaning together and when room cleaned so well, then Vasant said "Thankyou brother" and with a mischievous smile he said "big brother, I need some money to buy a video game, do you buy me that?", Vasant give suspicious smile and said "oh, that is why you agreed so easily to help me, but okay done", he screamed out in happiness and runaway back to his room and then Vasant make phone-call to Chitra and when she picked up Vasant said, "Chitra are you ready?", Chitra said "yeah", Vasant replied "okay Now come to my home", Chitra said okay, within an hour I will be there", and then Vasant started decorating, but he was a little confused, so he started with balloons, where he decorated all the space with balloons and clung pastel-coloured balloons all over the space. And then over the old brown table, he put a beautiful tablecloth of pink and white, which looks more beautiful because it has a white frill border that gives a vintage look to the table. Then Vasant found the lights were very dim, so he went to his and took all the fairy lights and scattered them all on the edges of the room floor. It gave a glow to the room that was missing before. After that, Vasant drew the letters on the chart and cut them out, and with the help of those letters, he made the word love. He filled in the red colour in the letters and then stuck them on the wall with the help of tape. After that, he has some paper flags, which give a graceful look to the whole room, and then he goes fast and dresses up well and puts the cake on the table, and this is how the whole space looks astonishing. Vasant makes a phone call to Chitra, but due to bad connectivity, they barely hear a word from each other. After that, his Brother comes and says, "A girl is waiting outside our house; are you waiting for her?", and Vasant rushes and says, "Yeah," and then he goes to the gate to pick her up, and Vasant now guides her to that backyard, and Chitra sees that amazing, astonishingly decorated room. She just felt it; her heart is on another level. She is looking at everything, and then her eyes fall on the beautiful tablecloth, where the table was looking like a pink and white rose. But when she looked at the cake, she felt amazing. Chitra looks at each and every balloon, and on some pastel-coloured balloons,

Vasant has made ugly and funny faces. Chitra gets so impressed by the way things are arranged and decorated so authentically, and with fairy lights, the place looks like a fairy tale for her teenage self. Although the persona of the eyes pursues thoughts to the soul, it will depend on the perception, where the perception of Chitra towards every effort of Vasant is love. she sit down on the chair and started gazing the cake, where she read out the message written on the cake "Will you be my soulmate?",and then she said "Yes I want to be your soulmate and love, that you will remember for years and years, you blow my heart with joy", and then with a shy face she said "put this ring in my finger", Vasant said "Chitra keep this ring up to you, I will put the ring in your finger, when I propose you to marry me, on our engagement, when I am going to wife you up and make you mine, infront of everyone. The feeling of putting a ring in your finger, on the engagement, I don't want to lose it, I don't want that, yeah, this is not something amazing because I have already done and feels like that". Chitra said "Really, this is a very unique thought process that I have ever heard of, but okay, I will wait for that moment", Then Chitra started looking at the shiny crystal of the ring and put it on her finger. Then she started daydreaming of their engagement, where she is in a beautiful gown, where her every feature are looking fabulous and heart-taking, where their families were sitting and every eye was waiting for the bridal girl, and when Chitra is coming, and everyone is watching her and only her. That moment running fast and slowly with light winds, that giving a great feel. And then in the gorgeous coat and pant, Vasant saw him coming with holding her hand and take her to the stage, and, looking at each other by opening the curtains of the eyes, and they put a ring in the finger, and everyone out there is clapping and hooting. with that the day dream ends.

Chitra said, "Although I knew it, I was too curious to listen to those words from you; it is a blessing to me. When everyone didn't find me, you were the one who did. In that search, someone who looks the way you look at me takes a lot of years to come to me, so I am always afraid that I will lose you". Vasant said, "Chitra, your worries. to my family I tell a lot about you. I respect your efforts to be mine, but don't worry, Chitra, I am here with you always. You enjoy and eat this delicious cake", After that, Chitra picked out her phone to take a selfie with Vasant. She clicked many selfies and photos of all the decorations that Vasant had done for her, including one of them together. Now that the photo time has ended, Vasant has started eating cake, where three-fourths of the cake alone is eaten by Vasant and Chitra eats the remaining one-fourth. This time, they can't hear the silence in their hearts. Their hearts are playing with the rhythm of the music. They are enjoying with full hearts and forgot about time in that sequence, and suddenly Vasant's mom started calling him on the phone because she is returning from her maternal house and she wants Vasant to come from his father's bike and take her back, and Vasant, when he suddenly saw the call of her Mother, she was scared, but with a shivering hand he picks up the phone and in confidence says "hello maa. So Mrs. Indra said, "What are you doing, my child?" and Vasant, with a shivering voice, said, "Yeah!!........., yes, mother, I am out for food", where Indra ji said, Okay, son, I will call you later, okay?" and she cuts the call. After that, they resume their celebration, and that is how the sweet day ends.

CHAPTER TWELVE

THE SWEET DAY

Now This day of Valentine's comes with sweet chocolates. Because they celebrate Valentine's week, which fascinates everyone about them, whatever they are doing towards each other has seemed like a dreamy story.

As for the weather, today is a little shady, and suddenly the black clouds get removed and it gets a clear blue sky that makes mountains visible out there. Yesterday it was raining, which is why today the cloud vanished and it looks clear. After that, a beautiful rainbow is visible in the sky, with five beautiful colours. Two colours were not visible, but the whole scene looks like the scenery of a beautiful valley. The trees are still covered with dew, and that gives Vasant an idea for surprising Trisha. He started planning how he could make her day special because just giving her chocolates looks easy and simple, and Vasant wants to change the dynamics of the day. So he attended the First two lectures, and Vasant dropped his further two lectures. Chitra saw where he was going, but she knew that he had something in mind; otherwise, he must ping her, so she kept doing the lectures, and other classmates were feeling weird about this. Because he knew that day was really special, he left her, and after that, he went to the destination and started preparing and decorating for her so that when he takes her there, she will see his efforts to make her day special. Every other student is spreading rumours that he must be going to take her on a date today, and everybody is so amazed by that. On the other hand, Vasant picked up Chitra directly after the class and said "I want to take you out by now", but Chitra said, "Yeah, let's go! But everyone is making rumours about us. Vasant started saying, Chitra, let them think; if you go or don't go, that is not going to change their opinion about us," and Chitra rethought and said, "Yeah, okay, although I am really very excited for your surprise, you know you are making me feel amazing and special. and she gets full of energy and excitement that she is going to get that happiness that only a few girls get. His love is jumbling in the arena wherever they go; for them, this world is under the influence of the music of love and like a loop that is never going to end. It seems Chitra's fortune was rewarding her for her simplicity and goodness. This time Vasant takes her to a dark, remote forest, and her whole emotion, Chitra, has been converted into fear. Where her brain is advising her not to go inside. It may have been a trap, but she blocked her thought process and started blindly following him. Her fear was genuine. Because Vasant has taken her into that dark forest, what are his intentions and motives? It might be good, but the fear in her eyes is briefing everything, and that's why Vasant took her there so early because it gets dark after a few hours. Vasant recognised her fear and tried to scare her more, because it was a tendency that, if a person is scared, even small things make them more scared. Vasant, making a scared face, said, "Chitra, see something is behind you," and she got nervous and scared and cried, "What is there, Vasant?" and got to cling to Vasant. Vasant felt even happier with this crazy moment, and with a giggle, he said "Chitra, see, there is nothing like that, and don't get scared by this forest because I am with you and I will not let any problem or thing even touch you", and that awakened the soft corner of Chitra. Now she is feeling more comfortable. Chitra is still afraid of some animals, but now Vasant is in her heart. Chitra noticed that when every place is looking a little dusky, there is one place that is full of lights. that is coming by passing from the canopy, and when Chitra reached the venue, she realised that a small area is decorated with flowers and handmade things, where in the centre is a big beautiful chart where with the colourful alphabets there is written "For my love Trisha, Happy Chocolate Day," and there is a wooden table, where in a beautiful brown bamboo basket there is a chocolate bouquet. There are so many chocolates and chocolates of different types. This looks so attractive to her, and she just loves the way that everything is arranged, where some trees are covered with lights. Chitra was now speechless. Vasant said "See, Chitra, with dusk, the rainbow is almost gone," and Chitra nodded her head and said "This surprise is so beautiful, and that light, that chart, that basket—everything that you arrange for me is appreciable, Vasant". They hugged each other after Vasant put out his Camera. Vasant started taking photos of Chitra and everything. It becomes so special and memorable, and after that, Chitra packs all the things into her memory and packs the gifts, chart, and chocolate into her bag. They have enjoyed themselves, and now they are returning home. On the other hand, In the train of the brain, Nishad is running fast, and he was thinking, "Vasant must be celebrating with Chitra; I will call him on Valentine's Day." Vasant has yet to update anything about him for today; he just can't ask Chitra, and he gets rumours from friends that Vasant has planned a surprise for Chitra. He bunked the class, and after some time, Chitra also get disappeared. They have gone somewhere, and no one has any idea about that. So Nishad made a missed call and started waiting for him to call back by himself. After an hour, Vasant, with a smile and a smitten heart, eats Chocolate and checks his phone. Now Vasant calls back, and now he picks up the call. Now Nishad asks Vasant, "So how are you, my friend? From many days I have noticed that you are too busy with your girlfriend and you don't give a single minute to me, you rascal". Vasant says. "You already know this is Valentine's Week, and that's why I am spending more time with her", Nishad says, "This is not right, Vasant; he has eaten up my time". Vasant replied sarcastically. "Your jealousy picks up words, Nishad", and after hearing this, they both started laughing, and Nishad got an opportunity, and he asked, "So tell me about your Valentine week?"

and he tells how he surprised Chitra and how he is celebrating Valentine's week. He tells about the innocent behaviour of Chitra and her love. He also says, "I have recognised her internal beauty and how loyal and beautiful a soul she has". Vasant can't stop appreciating her and her efforts. Chitra has an ambivert personality, so he is extroverted enough so that he can speak about her love but introverted enough so that he can't share any personal talk about her. On the other side, Alisha also called Chitra to learn about the first Valentine's week. Chitra is an extroverted person, and she gets really excited when she gets a phone call from Alisha. She picked up her phone and started talking to her, where she also asked Chitra about her Valentine's week, and Chitra started telling everything in a reel and each and every moment that happened. She tells about how much enjoyment they have had, how much effort Vasant has made for her, and everything regarding her love life. Alisha listened to the whole talk very happily, and she was really happy for her, and she said "Chitra, take care of him; if anything wrong happens between you and him, try to sort it out; don't just give up on each other, okay". Chitra said "Yes, sure, even if I face any problem, I will try to sort it out; otherwise, I will tell you, because you are my best friend". This is how this sweet day ends.

CHAPTER THIRTEEN

FOR A CUTE BEAR

The lights of the lover's festival were on the faces of every couple, and the trend these days is at a very high pace. Chitra's friend Alisha has a cute teddy bear that her boyfriend gifted her. So that was the centre of attraction in Chitra's eyes. In the past, she was always fascinated when she saw any teddy bear—a brown furry bear—that felt soft and cute to Chitra's eyes. At that time, she wished for that cute bear; although in childhood she had several toys, now as an adult, she wants that from someone special. That day has come. This is the reason for her happiness, and in comparison to other days today, Chitra has a lot of expectations for this day. She had especially waited for this day for a long time. She always felt that her companion was missing, and that teenage dream was something that she always wanted. After that, she gets ready, and she goes out in a beautiful purple suit and salwar with her traditional, beautiful Kashmiri art purse. She dressed and set up her outfit so perfectly that it is neither too highlighting nor dull; she especially looks pretty in this colour. She does little makeup, and she just looks simply gorgeous. She texted Vasant that she would reach the location by two 'o'clock so that he could catch her at their fixed place. Vasant borrowed his friend's motorcycle, and Vasant also dressed him up like a gentleman. Then he reached and saw Chitra standing in her beautiful purple outfit, and Chitra saw that today Vasant came here with a motorcycle. She was amazed, and Chitra was so happy while she was sitting on the back seat of her boyfriend's motorcycle. She is excited to be sitting in the back seat. While driving, Vasant is looking at her with the help of the side mirror and noticing her. When Chitra saw him like that, she gave him a shy look, smiled, and said, "Vasant, what are you looking for?", Vasant excused her by saying "Nothing, I am just driving". Chitra said, "I don't think so; I guess you are looking somewhere else," and Vasant just smiled and put on his shy face for her. While reaching there, her hairs were playing with the wind, and that is looking so attractive to Vasant. He just wanted to capture it on his phone, but clicking pictures at that time was a little hard, so he captured it in his eyes. Travelling on the bike with Vasant makes Chitra feels so excited, and they slowly reach the picnic point. Chitra doesn't want that bike to stop; she doesn't want to end it, but every beautiful thing has an end. When they reached there, Chitra and Vasant found how symmetrically everything was decorated there. Even though there are a lot of oak trees, few people sit under them and enjoy themselves with their families. Some of them are couples. On one side, they decorate their 'picnic point' with beautiful small huts that have barely a chair and table, but the simplicity of that valley makes it look amazing. Near this beautiful picnic spot, there is one hanging garden where the whole place is just holding nature. A small, beautiful, colourful terrace garden. Vasant asked Chitra "Would you also like to see the tea valley, a few kilometres away from this place?", Chitra said, "Yeah, I really love to see them, but we will go there only if time allows. "I wish it did not get dusky at that time," Replied Chitra. Vasant said, "Well, it's a choice, but yeah, your opinion matters to me". Chitra said "Oh wow!!... that's so cute; let's go, Vasant, can we go to sit in a beautiful hut?", Vasant said "Yeah, sure, my love, I have already booked it for you", and when Chitra heard that, she became so happy and started running to go over there. Because that place was not so crowded, Chitra didn't feel shy about stupid and funny little things. So Vasant also started running with happiness. And then Chitra asked, "Which hut do you book for us?", Vasant pointed out that hut and said, "That one on the corner side. When Chitra entered that hut, she found a cute brown teddy bear with a red bow tie. and he's looking so graceful in the eyes of Chitra. At that point, Chitra now becomes double jolly because, from her perspective, this is what she has wanted to feel for a very long time. Sometimes good things come a little late. That feeling was truly special because she believed in it and manifested it that day. Now that day is standing in front of her. It looks so normal to people, but for her, it has become so special because those little moments are what she is searching for everywhere. Chitra said, "Whenever I see soft toys of my friends that are mostly gifted by their partners, I feel that I also need one, so once I took my mother to that shop to buy it for me, and she refused and said that you already have one, but that was a soft toy, but I want the brown bear. Once I became so stubborn, and I collected my pocket money for that one brown bear, but when I went to the shop to buy it, I just felt like I didn't want to buy it on my own, that I wanted someone else to buy it for me; most probably a guy should buy it for me, and from that day on, that special day has come". After that, Vasant replied, "Oh, my Chitra, I know you are feeling happy and nostalgic at the same time, and I can also feel that. I am so happy that you liked it". They hugged each other, and then Vasant said, "Okay, now tell me, what should I order for you?" Chitra called the waiter, and the waiter said "Please, ma'am, tell me what you would like to order.", So Chitra said, "I want to order a burger, and Vasant, what about you?" Vasant said, "Only a burger? Are you dieting?" and then he said to the waiter, "Two egg rolls also, green kabab, and two majitos." The waiter took their order and said, "Thank you, sir, for your order; we will take a few minutes, and after approx. fifteen minutes, he served the food. They started discussing, enjoying, and eating like this. They spent a beautiful, quality time together. At the end of the trip, a question came into Chitra's mind, and she said, Vasant, how will I carry this teddy bear to my room?", So Vasant said to Chitra, Don't put so much load on your brain; this is my headache", so Chitra said "Okay". She put some courage in her and smiled, then Vasant dropped Chitra off at her flat. Chitra captures the pictures with her teddy bear, and a beautiful, prosperous day ends.

CHAPTER FOURTEEN

PROMISES IN HEAVEN

Now the glooming blue sky turns darker, and the next day is arriving, and this day is "Promise Day". This day is the gist of any relationship, because love is a promise. Chitra is excited about this day, and she awakes at three in the morning. Because it's so early, she lights up a candle and sits near the window of her room to observe the things around her, where in the little pieces of light, everything is looking faded. The trees and the grass in the backyard, that street light, that wind At that time. Chitra realised that even in the moonlight, things look more aesthetically beautiful, just like living under the influence of dark academia, dark but somehow touching the heart, just like a song with a soothing melody. She thought at midnight, "What can I promise him? Thoughts in her mind are coming: Well, I want to say that I stay forever with you, but one day we will die and then we get separated. Oh, Chitra, why do you always think like that? She thought of something positive, influential, loving, and unexpected. Something like that I can promise; yeah, I have nothing in mind that makes me feel special about this day, so for that I have to buy a gift at least, but what should I buy for promise day? It is sort of confusing to buy gifts. Okay, I will decide that in the shop. I guess that will be better for me. I want to make a lasting promise. I will try to speak the best words that I can obey and that I am going to give him. I will obey that my whole life, anyhow. I have to convince my parents for him; this can be the best promise. Why have I just fallen in love with him? Why, at that time, am I not able to control my feelings and let them flow? Maybe this is a gift from an angel. Suddenly, it started feeling like a deep breathe. Everything outside that window started looking like a painting. The frosty, freely falling water droplets sitting over the green grass and leaves in the form of dew and the Rainy weather have changed something in the heart of Chitra. She started watching daydreams in which she was dancing in the Rain with him. In that, she also sees those mesmerising eyes that love to see Chitra. She was daydreaming that Vasant was staring at her when she was dancing in the rain. In that sense, she just lived a lot more. After that, she blew out the candle and went back to sleep.

Sometimes we live more in imagination and less in reality. Those daydreams are actually more beautiful than any reality.

In the morning, when she awoke, she saw a message from Vasant in which he texted, "Good morning, Chitra, please wait after class for me. She got full of joy, but without showing any excitement, she texted back to Vasant "Yeah sure!", They both put the phone on the table and started preparing for the day. After that, they both go to the classes, and both are just counting seconds in class because they are eagerly waiting for each other and have great excitement in their hearts. Chitra is really curious about what Vasant has planned for her, and Vasant is also excited for his present. They were sitting in the class, imagining each other and thinking about what they should promise. After some time, the wait has now ended.

Class ends now, and Vasant and Chitra are trying to make eye contact by avoiding everyone.

Now When everyone is going home, Chitra and Vasant are going for the date on promise day, where Vasant said, "Today I am going to take you to that surprising place; would you like to go there?" and Chitra said "I will surely want to go with you". There are only a few people there, mostly couples, and Young teenagers just go there for romantic dates. Vasant has saved his pocket money for this Valentine's week, and he planned the whole week smartly by keeping things in the budget. He is a little smarter at managing money than most people are. Under sensational lights, they sat on the porch of that cafe, where the lighting and decoration were stunning. Where they promised each other something strange that they didn't expect, but they both felt that closure that was taking them towards each other. Vasant said to Chitra, "You will be mine even if this world separates us, because after my mistakes, I have learned a lot, and I chose you over everything. I am going to accept you and your every Scar". Chitra said "I will always love you, even if death takes you away from me, and I am always going to choose you", These words are pretty random, but somehow that was the great expression and feeling of love.

That place looks like heaven to both of them when they are promising each other. For Chitra,it was just like a fairytale that came true. She thought, It's more desirable that now someone has accepted me with my scars and whoever I am. Nothing shines more beautiful than the thought process when two true souls become a single entity. That day, Vasant and Chitra were shining in this way. and this is how another sweet day ends.

CHAPTER FIFTEEN

A LOVE GESTURE

The day changed with the theme and also with the weather. Today the clouds are grey and there are vultures in the whole sky, but the weather is less dusky than the place that Vasant has chosen for this Kiss day of Valentine's week. because they are now more familiar and know each other's comfort zones, there is no problem or nervousness. Now Vasant started thinking, and he was talking to himself in his thought: Well, with one kiss, I didn't make her feel special because we kissed each other several times, so how do I make her feel special? Well, can I buy something for her?, No no!!......... This is not going to work. oh god!! There is nothing in my mind, think Vasant; she is very special for you and I really want to make her feel special. I think I can take suggestions from a female friend because they can suggest something good. Well, I have to check with whom I should call! Oh, I think I have to ask Rashmi; she has quite good knowledge in this area, but she judges people a lot; I can't make her judge Chitra. Well, then I can ask my cousin sister Payal; she cares about her, and she won't judge me for asking that, okay? Now Vasant called Payal, and she picked up the phone and said "Hey brother, how are you?", Vasant replied "I am good, Payal, my sweet sister, can I ask you a favour?", Payal replied, "Sure! Sure! Tell me". Vasant said, "You know about Chitra. Today on kiss day, I want to make her day special; I have no idea regarding that, because just kisses can't make this day so special; for her, that's something she can remember", Payal gets shy but jolly and laughing voice, she said, "Well I don't know, Kisses aren't enough?........, but..........but, if you want something more special, take her out to a beautiful location. You can gift a loving couple gifts, or you can also design a theme cake for this day, like a fondant couple kissing each other. Did you like any one of them?". Yeah, you are right, and I love all of those ideas. I implemented all of them. Thank you, Payal, my loving sister. Now I have to go for further preparation. I will call you again! ... and thanks!", Payal replied, "Okay brother, have fun! Now Vasant started preparation, and after all the arrangements,he called Chitra and said, "Get ready; I am coming to pick you up." Chitra was thinking, Who cares about this day? What can he do to make it special? We will kiss, and that's it and it that we do commonly, still what else a person can do". After that, Chitra gets ready. She wore a dress that was dark and mysterious, like a canopy of night. She wore her black boots and made a breed from her hair, and she's looking stunning and remarkable. On the other hand, Vasant is preparing him for the day with the black T-shirt and jogger so that he will look like a cool and stunning guy. Vasant goes out to pick up Chitra. A shopkeeper near that place was noticing them daily, and they are now sure that they both are in an affair, but he has nothing to do with that fact, and that shopkeeper said to Vasant, "Oh, you come to pick up madam," and Vasant laughed and A shopkeeper near that place is noticing them daily, and they are now sure that they both are in an affair, but he has nothing to do with that fact, and he said to Vasant, "Oh, you come to pick up madam," and Vasant laughed and said, "Yeah!". That shopkeeper was thinking about their family and how their status, behaviour, activity, and clothes all define what their status is, but that is something that they both don't ever think of because they are in love.

Chitra was waiting there for Vasant, and when he came, they surprised each other because they were looking perfect together. Chitra sits on the back seat, and they both get vanished, leaving the winds, clouds, and everything behind them. This amazing speed of Vasant was the greatest thrill for Chitra. She had for the first time seen another amazing person hidden in Vasant, but there is still a lot more about him to see. Because now the roads are steep and they are making a trajectory, the bike started struggling somewhere to go upside down, and then Vasant struggled to slow down the bike to safely drive it. Now that she was noticing everything, a question arises in her mind. and Chitra asked Vasant, I want to ask something", because he doesn't want to divide his mind, and because that place was too steep, he is worried that one mistake can turn into an accident. Also While driving due to the wind, he is unable to hear anything, so he ignores her for sometime and first reaches the safe roads, and after that, he stoped his bike there and says, "Now you can ask", Chitra says, "I also want to learn how to drive a bike or a scooter; will you help me out?", Vasant replies, "Of course, Chitra, but in this critical situation why are you asking me this thing?, and, do you know how to ride a bycycle?", Chitra replied "I knew, but I am not confident enough to ride a bycycle on a crowdy road; I only have to do cycling on the ground and on empty roads", So Vasant said, "Oh, then it will be fine, because if you know how to drive a bicycle, you can easily drive a bike or a scooter. I think you don't only know how to handle the scooter in the rush; when you start facing the crowd, you get used to it, and I will help you".

Chitra becomes so happy with it, and they both start noticing beautiful greenlands and floral areas because that place was over mountains, and that was a thrilling place. Chitra was enjoying herself, and she was also navigating him through the boards. Then there comes a beautiful tea stall with the name "Quick Tea Point,", so Vasant and Chitra stop there. They sat down on the stool and ordered two teas, where the husband and wife who are serving the tea. there acute small boy who was looking from the wooden window, and Chitra, when she sees him, passes a smile, and the child playing with his pet comes out and stands in front of Chitra and Vasant. She started talking with him. basically small talks,but because that boy was so shy, he just stood there without saying a word. So he goes to his mother. Vasant and Chitra started enjoying their tea. The flavour of the tea was amazing in the mountains;

even there, you can't calculate the love of people for tea. That tea point was so popular there. After enjoying the tea and paying the bill, they continue their journey. While navigating Chitra, they accidentally took the wrong turn, and they started moving further in the wrong direction on the roads. There, when they move forward and there comes a road that is too steep and the road is only made up of rocks and stone, while Vasant is driving on that road, he finds it to be very hard to drive on the gravel-stone-covered road. Then Vasant realises that it is getting scary. As part of his responsibility, he has taken a girl with him. So he said to Chitra, I think we are on the wrong route and it is consuming time", Chitra found a traveller on the bike coming from the opposite direction, so she told them to stop. They stopped and said, "Yes, is there any issue? and then Chitra asked, Where is this road going? The traveller told her, Well, there is an adventure theme park there, but it is about to close" . Vasant said, "I don't want to take this risk with our lives; even our families don't know about that. If something bad happens, there is no one who can inform them, so I think we have to go back". Chitra agreed and said "Yes, you are right, we have to go back; I am also worried about my parents", Vasant agreed and turned the bike. Where the plan has been cancelled and that somewhere hurts, Chitra and Vasant can feel the numb part of her heart, but still, something else is waiting for them. After riding four or five miles within the colours of flora and fauna, there is greenery all around, and, because they reach there by chance, there is a beautiful cottage hidden in the clouds, where they crossed it without even noticing, but now Vasant has noticed that beautiful place, and that cottage has an audacious name that makes Chitra surprise and jolly, and that is "THE OLD MOTHER STORY." Basically, that cottage was designed with a beautiful vintage cottage kind of structure, where there are beautiful waterfalls, and that sound creates some whisper in the sweet silence. That cottage was reserved in the memory of a woman who spent her whole life on social welfare activities. So that place has divine goddess vibes; that place somewhere serves pure vibes to all atmospheres. When

Chitra read about that, she felt so relaxed, and then they loved everything about that place. Some people say that place is a horror, and some people feel that they can feel the presence of someone in that house. Some people say that women are somehow weird, and she was a little suspicious in other people's eyes. But the thing that keeps their attention is the vintage aesthetic that they have maintained, and no one knows the truth behind the rumours. Vasant and Chitra went inside and booked the room. Vasant said to Chitra, Do you want to take some rest? Should we go into the room?", Chitra said Well, I am not tired; let's roam here; it's so beautiful outside", Vasant said Okay, wait here; I am coming in two minutes", When Vasant asked the Receptionist "I want to ask something", he replied Yes, sir, sure". Vasant asked him, "I want to ask for a celebration. Is it possible here", He replied, "Yeah, sir, it will take almost two hours for arrangements; guide me on the plan." Vasant said, "Okay, well, the plan is to decorate with flowers, balloons, and lights. a blueberry cake with a theme of kiss day and food". The receptionist said "Okay, sir, and don't worry, you can pay the bill anytime, and we're starting the decoration". Vasant said "thank you," and then Vasant went back to Chitra.

In happiness, Vasant and Chitra started revoloving all around in that cottage, and in one lonely place, Vasant decided to kiss Chitra. While roaming here and there, Vasant stopped Chitra by pulling her hand without making a noise. Just from his eyes, he explained everything to Chitra, but in shyness, her eyes halted, and she started looking down so that he wouldn't make eye contact with her. They were a little nervous, but then they come close, and then they start kissing, and it all feels like a light bubble of emotion that is flying in over the imaginary sky with a feather-soft touch, changing the emotional status of the mind like a frequent change in weather. All those feelings were memorable. and that kiss became very special for Chitra. Vasant tried to make it special for her, and that became reality just like a beautiful dream that she even never imagined. They were becoming special for each other. Now they feel more comfortable with each other. Some people believe kissing is something physical, but for Chitra, it is something like comfort, getting favoured, acceptance, fate in love, the psychology of becoming each other's part, an imaginary feeling of fate that she wants to turn into foreverness. Now, slowly, the clock is also moving its hands to not only change the day into night. So Vasant said, I have a surprise for you, and Vasant took her to the west wing garden in those cottages. There, Chitra saw that the place was beautifully decorated for her; she got shocked and hugged Vasant in happiness. They cut the cake, kissed each other, and then gave her gifts that were highly admired by Chitra. After that, they go back. Vasant drops Chitra at her room and gets back.

So now all the sky is covered with the darkness of twilight. The twilight is feeling like the whole sky was under a dim light candle, and after reaching home, Alisha makes a phone call to Chitra to ask everything, and then she asks, "How was everything?", Chitra says, "I am going to tell you everything. It feels like a teenage dream that comes true. From movies, whatever fantasy I have explored, I felt similar to that, just like a soothing love song, where I can feel myself as the main character. Everything felt beautiful, like the colours of the rainbow and the efforts that he showed me. Everything was breath-taking. Before him, I just found myself as a shrivelling flower, but with him today, It feels like I am blooming. There is a lot that I feel in that moment; it is hard to tell, but there is a lot", Alisha replied. "I know how it feels, but this feeling is really special," and then they ended the call. Now Vasant and Chitra started calling and continued enjoying each other's company. This is how this beautiful day ends.

CHAPTER SIXTEEN

CLING IN THE SWING

A day now appears in the Calendar of lovers, and the feeling of being hugged was so gentle and graceful that everyone wants to experience it. A few people also believe that lovers are meant only for cuddles. In their imagination, these things look like a door to heaven or something peaceful. It is something that perfectly fits in any brain; it doesn't require any special quality to be intellectual, dumb, or moderate. The special thing about this day is that people celebrate it every day. "A way to represent your love—these are the perfect words for this day. You can resist everything except this temptation. On this special occasion of love, the weather was a little hazy and calm, just like a hug. For this day, Chitra has chosen a beautifully printed frock with a tight pony, a little touch-up, and perfume. She found this day so casual because this is what she always used to do, but she also knew that Vasant still had something for her, so she calmly waited for her present without giving any expression. Today she was looking so hot that no one could ignore her. She really looked like a piece of heaven; her glow is charismatic. Vasant makes a phone call to Chitra and asks her Where does my princess want to go today?". Chitra said "Oh Vasant, it's so tiring today, because for the past few days we have been going out regularly", Vasant said "Really?", Chitra said "Yeah, I am not an outdoor person; can you plan something at home?", Vasant asked,

"At your room? She said, "Do you want to kill me? Of course at your place", Vasant said. "Okay mam". By getting that much respect, she laughed and said, "What a gentleman you are, Vasant, but because you are asking like that, my heart gets melted, so I thought we can go for a movie and on the back seat we can hug each other; that even looks so romantic to me. We will choose a romantic movie to watch. Vasant said, "But those places are so crowded; do you really feel comfortable there to hug me?" Chitra replied "If you have a better plan and place, you can tell". In reply, Vasant thought in his mind, "I think if in my attic there is a projector, there we can watch any movie together, and I will make other arrangements before she comes.". Vasant sneered in happiness and said "Well, you are tired of going out and it is simply a hug day, so okay, come, I will give you a hug, that's all" and then she felt very strange about that, and she started thinking "Oh, I wanted a surprise, well, it's okay", and she cut the phone call. Chitra was preparing for going out by taking every basic thing that she requires into her purse. where, on the other hand, Vasant prepares a cosy tent in his attic. Outside, she will set up the projector and other things that he requires, such as the board over the projected film. After that, he decorates the attic with fairy lights and other cute and beautiful stuff. He arranged all the edibles. So when Chitra came to his Home, she made a phone call to Vasant. The moment the phone rings, in a hurry, Vasant just goes out to pick up Chitra. Vasant saw her standing in the backyard, where Vasant's heart whispered loudly something in his ear: that Chitra was looked Exquisite and perfect. He said, "Chitra, you look exquisitely beautiful today". Chitra smiled and said, "You too dear......... Okay, now let's go". Vasant started guiding him and said, "Come here, my Trisha, let me take you to my attic," and they both moved forward, and Vasant guided her on every single step. Finally, when they reached there, Chitra got so surprised that there were jolly waves coming into her heart, and in enthusiasm, she sat down in the tent that Vasant had decorated for her. She asks Vasant, Who decorated this place so beautifully?", Vasant proudly says, "The person who is sitting beside you has decorated everything here, me!", Chitra says, "Really! It's so nice, Vasant". "Which movie do you like to watch? Can you tell me any specific genre?" asked Vasant. Chitra replied "I want to watch a Romantic movie". Vasant made a shy face and said, "Okay, then I will select this one. Do you want to watch 'The Last Train? because I think this one is Romantic and I have read the story? I think you are going to love this". Chitra said "Okay, well, I love to watch any Romantic movie with you, okay play it". Vasant made all the settings and started the movie. Vasant already has the idea of the story; he's just doing a great job of giving spoilers. In the beginning of tragedy, he tells about the turning point that was going to come. where Chitra suddenly stops him and says, "Vasant Don't give spoilers; I want to see it on my own". In between the movies, Chitra gets so lost within that movie, but Vasant is also lost, but only in Chitra. In between, one bold romantic scene strikes in their eyes, and that unexpected thing makes both of them feel attracted to each other. Both feel so grateful for each other. At that time, Chitra showed her urge to get a hug; her eyes expressed everything to him, and Vasant came forward, and they hugged each other. That feeling was so special and romantic. That they were both going to remember it till their last breath. Although the movie is slow and romantic, it still has some comedy scenes. She laughed so diligently and made fun of Vasant by comparing every funny thing with him, and Vasant opposed it all and made fun of her in the same way. There were endless laughs and romances that she experienced. When the movie ends, Vasant asks, "How's the movie, Chitra?" She just hugged him and then said, "This movie is the best, because that was really so romantic to me, and watching that with you is a great loving experience. They already capture each other in their habits; that is what those days are actually made for, and this is what happens between both of them. Chitra looks into his eyes; it looks like she is just lost in those eyes. With the wind of love, she wouldn't be able to control herself and just kissed Vasant on the cheek. This thing made him happier than ever. The things he really wanted to express are hallucinating in the air. But Vasant said "No,

Chitra, no more kisses, okay? I didn't want to lose the special feel of kiss day; save it for the next day, okay", Chitra smiled and said "Okay, okay, I am not going to spoil it", Then Chitra asked, "Can I get one sweet tea of spring? I can feel this weather is so typical to feel; it is so different". Vasant sneered then said, "Chitra wanted tea; okay, let me make tea for you; you should wait for a few minutes here". This is the first time that she feels that much intimacy and closeness towards someone. She just never imagined how much she was feeling. In all the feelings, she lost all the moments. Vasant came up with the cup of tea and addressed that cup to her, and within a sip, Chitra realised he must have good cooking skills, and she asked, "Vasant, I guess you are a good cook. Am I correct?". Vasant said "Of course ", and his cheeks turned red, and he started dancing in happiness. She said to him, "This personality of yours is my favourite one from now on." Vasant said, "Oh, really," passed a smile, and sat down with her. Chitra's beliefs about intimacy were retro, but she still wants everything that Vasant wants. She felt she was sitting in the castle of love, with the passing of time making it stronger day by day. For Chitra, each day of Valentine's was a realisation, and the purity of her feelings in expressing her love is such a truth. Vasant, there is something that might be hidden in you, that I have absorbed from you, that thing making you love me even though I have too many scars; I must be a nobody who can be perfect for you, but I must be that nobody who searches you in every peace of day," said Chitra. Vasant feels so proud of these words; his eyes are open, and he feels the goodwill of sitting beside her. Somewhere, it awakens the ego's desire to be perfect in everything, but he was not sure if he was the perfect lover or not. These kind words of Chitra assure him that these things are what he is made up of. He decided to boast about being a perfect lover in front of Nishad. Now Vasant said to Chitra, "Don't you see outside; it is getting dusky. See from the window; it is time to go back to where Chitra didn't want the day to end. Chitra said, "Yeah, I have seen the time; it is getting too late; now I have to go. Vasant smiled and said "Yeah.". Chitra's eyes widen in happiness.

After that, all conversation broke into small talk, and he dropped Chitra back in her room. After that, Vasant has a long to-do list for his work and office. Chitra started arranging everything, and within that, the whole day ends.

CHAPTER SEVENTEEN

WILL YOU BE MINE?

With each step of Valentine's ladder passed, They finally reached the rooftop of "Valentine's Day". Where there was actually a saint named "Valentine", he was a Roman saint who was a martyr for his beliefs in love and simplicity. He used to spread among people. There is a great reverence for his sacrifice, and even in the Roman Catholic Church, saints and other people commemorate him. Because February fourteen was the day of his martyrdom, on this day the priest commemorates him, and slowly, through his faith in love, it spread more and more. This is how this day has started, as we are living history, so this is how it comes in the fortune of Vasant and Chitra. They have decided to celebrate this day. Valentine's Day is the story of millions of lovers. Some end their lives together, some lose their love early, some get cheated because love doesn't work every time, and some love fades. Sometimes people use other people for their status and money, but there are a lot more that are just intuitions that are calculated as love and sometimes just infatuation. Everyone has their own love story; some believe in it and make it work out, and some enjoy it just for a moment and let it vanish in the sky of stories. They pretend that they don't have them and store them in frozen parts of their hearts. Some people, with time, become hollow, and their emptiness requires a love that they don't have, so they usually hate this day. Everyone has their own ground of perception for love. Where Chitra and Vasant are standing on the pitch of that love. It fascinates the eyes of a teenager, which is why Chitra has butterflies of excitement and hides from everyone. Chitra had already slept with the dream of her Valentine's Day. She woke up and found an anonymous smile. She went to fresh in the morning and came slowly with lazy steps, started looking in the mirror, and started observing her, where she just found her every flaw so beautiful and serene, sinking in the love melody that Vasant had played. She goes outside on the balcony, and she finds out that the weather is a little hazy and warm today. But it is quite romantic today; Vasant was also watering all the plants.

for this special day, Chitra wants to get ready and prepare well, and for that, she only relies on Alisha. So she took her clothes and went to Alisha's place. Where she says hello to the mother of Alisha and asks, Aunt, where is Alisha?" She replied "She is in her room; what would you prefer, tea or coffee?", Chitra replied "Thank you so much for asking; I usually prefer Tea", Alisha's mother replied, "sure!!, sit here; I will call Alisha and bring you a cup of tea." After some time, Alisha came down and said, "Chitra, sorry. Actually, I was in the bathroom". Chitra said, "It's alright". Alisha's mother served them tea and said, "My children enjoy your tea; I am going upstairs to clean the floor," and she went away. Alisha said, Yeah, now tell me the reason I let you come to my doorstep, and I guess it is about Valentine's Day, so finally you get Prince Charming, but yeah, tell me". Chitra smiled and said, "Yeah, you are right. Okay, let's go into your room. They went to Alisha's personal room, and then she opened her bag and said "I have only these two dresses for Valentine's Day; which one should I wear?", Alisha said, "Well, this one of yours is too funky and it will not give you an impressive look, but this one is too simple for Valentine's Day. So let me search in my cupboard, and Alisha selected some dresses. Then she said to Chitra, Go, let's wear these and show me; I will choose which dress you look perfect in.", So Chitra changed one after another, and finally, Chitra looked very beautiful in the red gown, and she also looked good in the eyes of Alisha. So Alisha said, "Yeah, you are looking perfect in this red gown, and it suits you more because it is a good outfit for your first Valentine's Day. Let me do a little touchup", Chitra started dancing in happiness in front of the mirror and thinking how pretty she was looking in this red dress. It was like being a fairy in the real world. So she sat over the wedge, and Alisha started doing her makeup. She decorated her with beautiful, shiny jewellery and gave her black boots. a beautiful pendant for her neck; she curled her hair a little and put some eyeliner and mascara on; now Chitra is looking super gorgeous, and now Chitra hugged Alisha for giving her a beautiful and amazing look. Alisha said "You are looking so beautiful" and then they started talking about Valentine's Day, and Alisha started giving advice to her for today, and in the end, she remembered the main point and said, "Chitra he was giving you surprises for every day, and you are receiving them; why are you not giving to him? He also has expectations from you at least on this", Chitra said, "Oh, you are right, but how foolish I am, I don't even think of that. Cause I am just expecting and that is wrong, but don't mind, I will do it on Valentine's Day". Alisha said "Let's go to the Gia Gift shop, where they find a quite decent shop". Chitra said "yeah, let's go". After that Chitra and Alisha entered the shop and started looking over the small gifts that were placed on the racks. There were so many couple gifts: string bags, keychains with different cartoons of couples, heart-shaped pendants, tumbler couples mugs with the words hubby and wifey, girlfriend and boyfriend, kin and queen, etc. There are greeting cards, earrings, chocolates, small beautiful diaries, cute soft toys, pendants, photo frames, watches, bracelets, romantic roses, and a lot more gifts.

Chitra feels jolly, and she wishes to buy all the stuff. Chitra asked Alisha, "What should I buy for him?", Alisha replied Well, I am not going to help you; I think you should buy something of your own choice, because you only know what kind of person he is and what he loves", Chitra, after five minutes of brainstorming, realises that Vasant is overall a romantic guy; he likes romantic stuff, so Chitra said, "He is not the boring one; he is crazy and a romantic one, so I think I have to buy something romantic. What about that snowglobe? It was playing quiet and calm music, even giving off a wedding feeling because the couple were standing in the snow in their wedding dresses. I think he likes this, and I always wanted to gift this to my soulmate, and I think he is the one", Alisha said. "Oh, why not? This is so beautiful, and you can see the colour combination is also very ethical". Chitra asks the shopkeeper, "Uncle, how much does this cost?" , The shopkeeper replied, "It cost one thousand and five hundred rupees, ma'am." Chitra said "okay" and then started picking out money from her pocket. Then Alisha said "Yeah, Uncle, tell me the right price for this snowglobe". The shopkeeper replied, Madam, it is the fixed price, and I am not going to give you any bargain; if you want to buy this, pay; otherwise, buy something that is cheaper in price; look at that couple sitting over the swing; it will cost seven hundred; you can buy that". Chitra said to Alisha "It's okay, this is an important day and the important gift, so it's okay" and finally decided to buy the snowglobe because she also wanted to fulfil her dream, so she said to the shopkeeper "I want to buy a snowglobe " and the shopkeeper said "Okay, madam" then Chitra said "Okay, and cover this with gift wrap", So the shopkeeper wrapped it with a shiny, beautiful printed design paper.

On the other hand, Vasant, after preparation, goes to his room to get ready. He looks in the cupboard, where he found the different colours of shirts and pants. He becomes so confused, and he tries all of them to decide what to wear because he has no idea what Chitra is wearing. So after brainstorming, he decided to wear a dark blue shirt and grey pants. He put on some perfume. Then he wore black formal shoes and ran out to pick up Chitra because she had three missed calls and she was waiting at Alisha's home. So Vasant was in a hurry to go and pick up Chitra. and she called when he was about to reach Alisha's home. Chitra said, "Thank you, Alisha, for making me feel so gorgeous, and now Vasant was near, so finally I am going on a date with my Valentine," and made a small giggle. Alisha said, "I am so happy for you, and enjoy your day!". When Vasant reached there and saw Chitra in that red gown, he felt that she was looking as beautiful as a rose. He felt crazy emotions, and he thought I would take a professional photo with Chitra and show that to Nishad to make him jealous. The lost souls finally reach the destination of this day, which was the most amazing and crazy place for a teenager. They celebrated each day with a different vibe, so for that special day, Vasant decided to bring something special to her, and for that, he first took her to the venue that he had reserved for her. When Chitra entered the hall, she found that the Balloon decoration and the whole room were covered with beautiful lyrics of her favourite song, which Vasant had mentioned earlier to the owner of that cafe, and some musicians were standing around and treating Chitra just like a queen. She really felt like a princess, and she was reminded of all the old days when she watched those things in the fairytale and that all things came true in front of her eyes. Then a waiter in an aesthetic kettle brings tea for them. where that waiter addressed Chitra as Mam, and Chitra liked that. Chitra was just taking a sip of tea when another waiter in Rajasthani traditional dress brought "chappan bhog," which is a big plate in a small bowl. There are 56 different things in every bowl. When Chitra saw that, he said, "Oh my god, it's so cool, Vasant. I am just surprised; these all things are unexpecting". Vasant smiled and said, "You just see what happens next". Chitra smiled in fondness and said, "Okay, I am really excited, 'cause things are going even more exciting than I thought". After that, two waiters came. They are holding a three-floor cake, which is a white cake covered as a whole with Vanilla cream, where the upper floor of the cake has a beautiful floral design, the second floor is covered with fairy lights, and the bottom of the cake has some heart chips and a boy and a girl giving hearts. where on the top of the cake two toys of a girl and a boy were sitting over the moon, and that cake was the best cake she had ever seen. Then she remembered that once, in front of Vasant, she said that she loved these floor cakes, and he kept that in his memory. Chitra found that very pampering. She felt that comfort under his shade and felt like everything was in their favour, feeling just like a queen there. She is going to remember her whole life. After that, two waiters came and took the table away, dimmed the lights, made that place feel like a private one, and played slow music. Chitra gets was surprised and said, Vasant, what happened?" Vasant stood and said, "Hey Chitra. Would you like to dance with me" Chitra first felt very shy and then replied Yes, why not", She stood and put one of her hands on her shoulder, and with the other hand, she held his hand. They started Dancing slowly and calmly. What a serene, beautiful moment that caught their eyes. That closeness made them feel special to each other. After enjoying that light music, they go back to their seats. Chitra said, "I don't know that you can dance like this", Vasant said "Yeah, Chitra, you know I am not predictable; you don't know about my hidden qualities". Chitra said, "Oh, I see. I love to see these qualities in you; now I can make other girls jealous of this fact". Vasant laughed and said, "Oh yeah, well, Chitra, I think now you have to cut the cake". Chitra said, "Yeah, sure". Chitra blow blows out the candles. After that, Chitra picked up the knife and said Vasant, hold this knife with me", so Vasant nodded his head and put his hand above Trisha's hand, and they cut the cake together. They started eating the cake, but they realised that it was so large after eating the desired amount. Chitra said, Vasant, now what do we do for the rest of the cake?", Vasant said, "No problem; I will take it home. I will Finish it with my brother within a few minutes, and if you want to take it to your home, you can". Chitra replied, No, no, I don't I am full". Vasant said, Okay, if you don't want to take it, I will take it for sure". After that, they order some street food, and after that, Chitra takes out the gift that she was hiding in the purse, and when Vasant sees that Chitra has brought a gift for him, he said, "There was no need to Bring a gift for me, Trisha, but you have brought it with so much love, so let's see what's inside", Now Vasant started opening the gift, and when he removed the whole gift wrapper, he opened the box and saw that Snowglobe". When Vasant saw that, he became so happy and hugged Chitra and said "Wow, this is so beautiful; it just looks like you and me inside this globe dancing on our wedding", Chitra replied to this comment. Vasant, I just love this white gown; I also want to wear it to our marriage function". Vasant said, "Why not, my love? I will bring you this, okay? This is the most delicate and beautiful gift I have ever received," and Chitra gets so happy after hearing that. After that, Chitra said, "Vasant, I am craving for some fast food; can you order?", So after that, Vasant ordered a spring roll and momos. They have enjoyed eating it together, and this is how, in eating, drinking, and small talk, the clock moves forward, and then Vasant Drops Trisha back to her home, and this is how Valentine's Day ends with a lot of sweet memories.

CHAPTER EIGHTEEN

FIRST ANNIVERSARY

Within that love, minutes turn into hours, hours into days, and days into years. years to a bunch of years, where they settle down. Slowly their love started glooming, and with their hard work and courage. After a long struggle, they convinced their parents. Vasant was very courageous and she never leave her alone and he request and too many times to the father of Chitra and in the last Chitra's father found him as a deserving Son in law. So fianally he said Yes to Vasant. They got married and Chitra turned into his wife, and the love for which he was looking everywhere is now with him, just like a dream turning into reality.

With the passing time, Now On their first Anniversary, when randomly Vasant and Trisha met, all the flashbacks came out that were in their heads, like this. Vasant saw Trisha after a long time, so it sounded like nostalgia. Trisha asked "So she is your wife?", Vasant replied "Yes and He? ", Trisha said " Yeah he is my husband". Trisha's face telling that she gone through a sad story. Vasant said "that was so great, so how that happens", Trisha said "it was different from yours, When our parents seperate us, I thought I never going to get the love, but when he comes and we gave time to each other, so I realise, that the love that I felt for you was so childish and stubborn, no doubt I have loved you alot, but the way he loved me was so different, I never forget your love, but it feels to be very different to be with him", Vasant said "that's so great", Trisha said "you don't tell anything about her?, although I m still jealous but tell", Vasant said " After you leave, I thought I am very lost, but when she came and she shared her tiffin and work with me,than I realise she is someone very different, genuine and kind. She became someone very important to me. We spend time with each other. But you remember what happened when we were long distance things separated us; similarly, we also jumped into a long distance thing. Chitra and I were still trying to date, and sometimes I completely push her away, causing issues in settlement and family problems. I was scared to bring her into the family because she was so loving, sensible, and kind. But the moment I pushed her away, I felt and realised that I loved her so badly that I would never find someone like her in the entire world. So I keep everything to myself because, at the moment, I realise I would never fall in love again until I found her, and those words change everything, and after that, I married her last year.We gone through same issues but still this time I am very sure, that I will make her mine and all other things, as you can see", Trisha said, "that's not fair, but that was good" and they smiled and said, "Good bye to each other!".

THE END!!

Thankyou so much to all my readers!!

I wish you fallen in love with this book!!